WILDMAN

A
NICOLE BERETTI
THRILLER

LUKA T. JACOBS

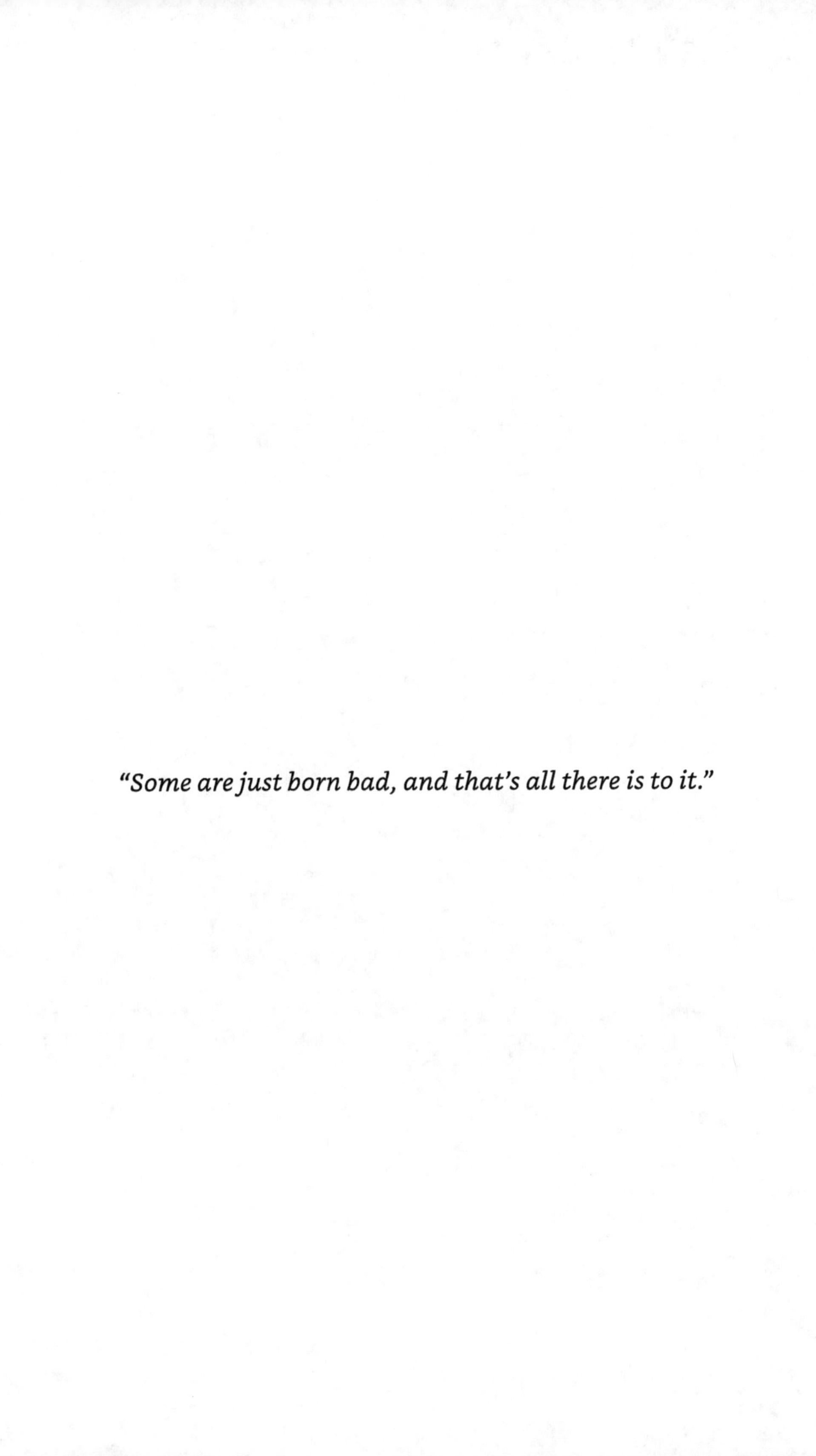

"Some are just born bad, and that's all there is to it."

FROM THE AUTHOR

Hi fearless readers!

I have wanted to bring my two favourite characters down under for a long time. In this book I finally did. New challenges, new scares, new trouble. Same type of antagonist, different land.

I hope you enjoy the ride and pick up a little Aussie slang along the way. Arvo, servo, bottle-o, ute. Say them out loud. Thanks for reading and for coming with me to this beautiful corner of the world.

Luka T. Jacobs

Follow on Facebook & join my newsletter for new books, extras, and cryptid goodies.

FB: https://www.facebook.com/lukatjacobs
A: https://amazon.com/author/lukatjacobs
W: http://www.LukaTJacobs.com

CONTENTS

PROLOGUE

They hit Bangera Dam most afternoons after work, two twenty-two-year-olds in a tinny with two oars, a faded esky, and a towel that never quite dried between trips. They had closed out the registers at the supermarket, peeled off their polos in the staff room, and driven straight here for a few hours of freedom. Maddie liked to stretch out and chase a tan she swore would finally stick. Jamie brought a book and a wide-brim hat Maddie had mocked once and then borrowed twice. They knew the launch, the shallow shelf, the way the trees leaned close around the bank. It felt like their secret spot.

Maddie lay along the bench seat, one knee up, sunnies on. "He texted me again," she said, phone face down like that might slow whatever was in it.

"Which one?" Jamie asked, eyes on her page.

"Lenny with the ute. Thinks he's the gift. Sent a selfie with his dog like it makes him deep."

Jamie smiled into her book. "Maybe the dog is the selling point. What did you send back?"

"Nothing yet. Might ghost him. I reckon he'd live."

"Reckon he'd write a song about it," Jamie said, and Maddie made a noise that meant please don't.

They drifted with the oars resting along the gunwales, the bow pointed toward a clean run of sandstone where the bank lifted straight to the water. A dragonfly tracked them, lost interest, and skated off. Somewhere in the reeds a moorhen complained.

Jamie read the same paragraph twice and let it go. Maddie breathed like someone about to nap, one hand loose on the towel. They had been friends since school and never ran out of nothing talk. They could sit for an hour and have it still feel full.

Jamie looked up from her book and glanced past Maddie toward the bank and froze. At first it was only the tree. Then it wasn't.

"Mads," she said, barely above a whisper.

"What?"

Jamie didn't point. Something at the back of her neck said don't. "What is that?" she asked, and her voice thinned. "Is that a homeless man?"

Maddie pushed up on her elbows and followed Jamie's eyes. On the bank about seventy metres off, half hidden by a bloodwood trunk, something stood on two feet. Dark hair lay over it, near black where the shade cut it. Taller than any man they had ever seen, even the footy boys when they crowded under the pub light. Hair hung long over the head and half masked the face. The frame was lean and hard, muscle without softness. Where the hair thinned the skin showed charcoal grey. It didn't shift. It didn't fidget. It faced the water and the part of the water where they floated.

"I don't know what it is," Maddie said, prickles running under her sunscreen. "But it is creepy as fuck."

Jamie's heart hammered. "Grab an oar," she said. "Let's move away. I want space."

They picked up the oars together. No splashing. Smooth dips and pulls to avoid making it obvious they were alarmed. The tinny edged out from the bank. Maddie watched the shape through the corner of her glasses. It didn't step. It didn't follow. It watched them make distance.

"Middle," Jamie said. "Go to the middle."

"I'm going," Maddie said, and because her mouth ran when she was spooked she mumbled something about charging admission if blokes were going to stare.

Jamie didn't laugh. "Please don't," she said. They set the boat where the water ran deep and turned slow.

When they looked back, the shape was gone. Only trunk and rock and light. Maddie let out a breath. "That was weird."

"Yeah," Jamie said, quietly as she scanned the bank. Her palms were damp on the oar. "Should we go?"

Maddie held the shore in her sight. "We'll be fine out here," she said. "It's gone. I'm not paddling back because some creep wanted a look. Twenty minutes, then we head in. Okay?"

Jamie didn't love the plan, but she liked being brave next to Maddie. She lifted her book and looked for the page she was up to. The bank moved to the back of their thoughts.

Ten minutes slid by. Jamie thought about taking a selfie,

put the book down, lifted her phone, then set it on the towel. Something brushed the tinny below the waterline. Soft, like weed. She glanced down and told herself not to be silly.

A delicate splash followed, like a pebble dropped a metre from the hull. She looked for the rings and didn't see them because they were already opening under their reflection. The hairs along her arms lifted.

"Mads," she said, and Maddie grunted, half annoyed.

Something broke the surface beside the tinny, rising in one smooth push: dark hair slicked back over a skull too broad for any person, black eyes set deep and far apart, a mouth impossibly wide with teeth bared. Water poured off in sheets as it drifted within reach, close enough to touch. Jamie screamed, sharp and high, the sound bouncing off the water while her book slid from her knee and tapped her ankle.

Maddie turned, saw it, and made a sound she had never heard from herself. The thing lifted an arm with speed that ate the space. The hand was huge and long, hair stringing off the forearm. Fingers closed on the rail and then on Maddie's wrist. One pull and she came off the seat and hit the water in a splash that slapped the tinny.

Jamie scrambled to the far side, knees smashing the esky.

"Maddie," she yelled once, voice high and torn. She lunged for anything and grabbed air. Her head filled with one order. Make yourself small. She folded in, head down, rocking back and forth, whispering, "It's going to go away. It's going to go away," over and over as the tinny drifted.

Long minutes stretched with only the slow turn of the boat and the small chop against the hull, the silence working on her until it felt like it might split her open.

The tinny heaved up from beneath, hard, like a buried fist driving into the hull. It lurched half out of the water, tipped, and threw Jamie over the side. Cold closed over her and the world became bubbles and weight. She kicked and broke the surface, gasping, hair in her eyes, the boat turning slowly beside her. Terror clamped her chest. She cried and spun, searching the water and the bank.

Something huge clamped her ankle and yanked. The joint popped with a white flash, and whatever sound she had left was swallowed as she went under into dark water where the light thinned and everything turned to pressure.

CHAPTER 1

FBI Special Agent Nicole Beretti guided the rental car down Highway 12 while rain stitched the pines into a gray sheet and the wipers kept a steady rhythm that left just enough clarity to hold the line through the bends. She had just left a small station where the local sheriff walked her through several recent reports that could possibly be a cryptid but nothing concrete yet, and they agreed it did not need resources at this stage; Beretti said she would pass the notes to analysts to track in case the chatter grew.

Her phone vibrated on the console. She took the next turnout, set the car in park, and answered on the second ring.

"Beretti."

"How are you, Nicole?" ASIC Ward asked, the check-in

brief and even.

"Good," she said. "Just met the sheriff. Nothing urgent."

"Good," he said. "I am sending you and Jacobi to Australia. Echo Creek, Queensland. Escalation in what many suspect is a Yowie. Australian Federal Police on board. Queensland Police briefed."

She watched rain slip down the windshield in thin ropes that caught the light from a passing truck.

"Australia," she said.

"Took work to set it up," Ward said. "I will send flight details. Wheels up from Boeing Field at twenty-two thirty. Case file will be on the plane. Call me from the tarmac."

"Understood," she said, and when the line went quiet she let the woods settle around her.

This should be interesting, she thought.

She pulled back onto the highway and let the long, steady bands of rain carry her toward Seattle. At a pump under a low canopy she added fuel, changed the GPS to King County International, and sent a text with her thumb resting light on the screen.

BFI 22:30. South gate check. Lucky you, you get to travel private again.

Jacobi's reply landed before the receipt printed.

Can't wait! Get to work on my tan. Smiley face emoji.

She slid back onto the road and let the city draw nearer while her mind ran through the last two months in a quiet roll that did not need words to carry it. She had spent long days at the old family house with a pry bar and paint under her nails, setting rooms in order so the place felt like it belonged to the living again. She had stepped out between those days to help end a war that never made the news and left its marks in timber and bone rather than headlines. She had stood in the dark where Red Eyes had once owned the night and finished what he began years ago when he took her parents, the work done with a steadiness she had not known she could hold until the moment required it. The roads since then had felt cleaner, the edges of sound sharper, and the knife at her hip had settled into a weight that matched the shape of her life.

Rain slipped across King County International as Beretti felt the familiar pull before an assignment, that steady lift of focus that always found her at the start of a case. Security waved her through on Ward's clearance, and the hangar pooled white light across wet concrete where a small jet waited with its door open and a ground tech nudged a chock with his boot.

Jacobi stepped from the shadow of a sedan with his go bag in one hand and coffee in the other, his focus on the private jet. When he noticed Beretti approaching, he lifted his coffee in a small salute and left his hood down while the rain tapped his jacket.

"You look excited," she said as they met at the stairs.

He glanced at the jet and let a small smile touch the corner of his mouth. "Ward pulled strings, looks like. Private again."

"Aren't we lucky?" she said. "I do not know what the case is about yet. The file is on the plane. We have plenty of time to go over it."

The pilot leaned from the door and gave them a nod.

"Agents," she said. "We are fueled and ready. Call it when you want to roll."

"How long are we flying," Jacobi asked as he ascended the stairs.

"About six hours to Honolulu with a brief fuel stop," the pilot said. "Then about nine hours to Brisbane."

He shook his head and let out a breath as he found a seat. "Guess I will catch up on some sleep."

As Beretti sat down, she pressed Ward's contact and kept her voice low.

"On board," she said. "We will lift in five."

"Good," he said. "Keep me posted."

"Copy," she said.

The jet was quiet but not sterile, its interior trimmed in dark timber and cream leather. A small bar stood along the left wall beside a half-moon counter stocked with bottled water and single malts. The cabin could seat sixteen, though only four were aboard today. Beretti and Jacobi were joined by two agents hitching a ride to another assignment. Beretti sat opposite Jacobi, both buckled as the plane steadied above the clouds.

When they leveled, Jacobi opened the case file. Photos and maps covered the screen and the seatback table. The first images were stark: a hunter's camp ransacked, the tent ripped to shreds; a trail bike on its side in the scrub, a dark pool of blood in the sanded track. The maps carried more weight. One showed the town grid and the gully that ran behind houses.

"Echo Creek," Jacobi read from the header. "Population two thousand eight hundred. No dedicated police station in town. Nearest is fifteen kilometers away."

Beretti traced the line from a shaded ridge to the edge of town. "Devil Monkey Mountain," she said, tapping the origin point. "It drops behind a vineyard, then follows a gully behind houses and eventually a school. If this reflects habit, that gully is a concealed approach into properties."

He flipped to the summary page. "Talk of Yowies and other things goes back as far as anyone remembers. People only started speaking up in the last two years. In five years, eleven missing. Three in the last two months. Hunters. One trail biker. Others tried a night in the bush for cryptid content and left at sunup. Some left town without a word."

She let the numbers sit. "Eleven from a town of two thousand eight hundred is not normal by any means. Three in two months is a major problem."

"Harassment list," he said, scanning. "Rock throwing, screams, banging on houses, yard equipment taken, animals mutilated. The usual. Reports get filed with the station in the next town. No one has been able to stop any of it."

He opened the referral trail. "This is how it got to Ward. One of our cryptid analysts in Colorado grew up in Echo Creek. Family still there. A cousin reached out. They are talking about selling the family property that has been in the family for more than a hundred years. They have tried everything they can think of. The analyst passed it onto their supervisor who in turn brought it to Ward. Ward called Australian Federal Police (AFP). AFP spoke to local authorities. Local police welcomed help. Out of options."

Beretti studied the map and the way the line slid past the school. "That path runs dangerously close to a school playground. That is an invitation waiting to happen. If Yowies are anything like Sasquatch, they are curious, and kids' laughter will draw them."

"Devil Monkey Mountain says enough," Jacobi said.

"I agree," Beretti said, glancing out the window.

He closed the laptop. "They must be desperate if they are calling us in."

Beretti nodded and set hers aside.

The jet held a steady line through the dark. Beretti slept in short blocks and woke to the same soft light and engine hum. She set a palm on her bag, felt the knife through the fabric, and let her breathing match the cabin's quiet. Time to trade the hum for heat, insects, and the work of putting things back in order.

CHAPTER 2

He kept to the cuts where water ran after rain. The ground there stayed cool and the brush stitched a shelter over him. The air held damp stone, leaf rot, and the slow drift of animal. Barkers were louder in the open. Here their voices thinned and broke, and he could slide off the trail and move past them without being seen. The wind told him who had walked ahead of him and how long ago. He trusted his nose more than his eyes.

He did not remember a time when he liked others of his kind. Their smell pressed in. They stared too long. He came out wrong and stayed wrong. His mother rejected him. The rest pushed him to the edge and then away from them. After that he moved on his own. Ridges. Flats. Creek runs that braided past the hard dens the hairless ones built. He travelled where the wind was clean and the scents read true.

No one taught him about thundersticks. He learned by pain. The first strike came from a low ridge with cattle. The air cracked and his shoulder burned and would not lift for days. After that he noticed the shapes that made that sound. Long sticks. Short ones at the hip. They carried a bitter unnatural scent, dry and sharp on the tongue. He watched how hands held them and learned to stay downwind. Without a stick the hairless ones were easy. Easier than mud-rooters. Easier than big red jumpers that could split him if he stood wrong.

Survival sat at his center. He ate what he found when he found it. Wild fruit on fence wire, sweet and warm. Small night-hissers that left a musk on his lips. Mud-rooters at the edge of water, rank and filling. Red jumpers when the dry bit hard. Barkers annoyed him, made noise, and tasted like old meat. Hairless ones when hunger and chance lined up. He did not like their taste. Thin and sour, unnatural scents on their skin, smoke in their hair, fear sweet-sour in the breath. He took them when anger ran high or when meat had been scarce too long. He ate enough and cached the rest in cool pockets under roots or stones where the ground breathed and flies had to search for a way in. He found water by its cold smell under clay, and he found meat by the iron that rose from it even in the dark.

He could move at night without brushing a leaf. He kept the wind in his face and the noise behind him. He could tap a stone on a post and hear a small one wake and a keeper hold her breath. He could smear high on the clear wall and know that in the morning they would point and talk and leave food in their pens, not to feed him but to keep something else busy. Fear did its own work and he used it. He liked the way it moved through them. He liked the stillness that came after.

He knew their signs. The eye on a pole that clicked and watched. The twin red pinpricks that blinked. The small box by a door that chirped when a hand pressed it. He learned to move where their eyes did not look. He learned that turning one eye a fraction made them argue later about wind and wiring and never about him. He learned which dens held barkers and those that didn't.

There were weeks when food came easy. Fruit dropped thick behind a fence. A mud-rooter bled out in a fight not thirty steps off his route. A red jumper broke a leg on the gully lip. In those times he stayed. When the run thinned, he left. He would take the mountain side, keep a ridge on his left or his right until the smell of water rose again. He did not think of it as leaving a home. The land either fed him or it did not.

The hairless ones who came for him carried the dry metal tang of thundersticks even when they hid them. He watched from cover, counted the sticks he could see, scented the ones he could not, and stayed downwind until the air told him to move.

He kept moving. He kept quiet. He read the land and the wind and let both read him back. If the land gave, he stayed. If it did not, he went.

CHAPTER 3

The jet door opened to heat lifting off the concrete. A lean brunette with a blunt bob waited at the foot of the stairs in a navy polo and scuffed boots, sunglasses low, jaw set. She looked fit, about twenty-six. "Afternoon. Officer Taylor Ellis with the Australian Federal Police," she said. "Call me Ellis. Beretti, Jacobi? Good. Grab your gear. Car's this way."

She walked them across the tarmac to an electric BMW iX with a charge cable coiled in the boot. Jacobi glanced at the badge, one eyebrow lifting, then slid into the back seat without comment. Beretti took the front and accepted a slim folder; the tabs matched what she had already studied on the flight.

"I know you've read in," Ellis said as the SUV glided out

through service roads and into traffic. "I'll hit the basics while we drive. No speeches."

They moved through suburbs that refused to thin. Warehouses handed off to shopping strips, then estates with new roofs and young trees staked under neat ties. Jacobi watched it roll past and let the window carry his voice. "First time here. Not what I pictured. I get you guys drive on the other side, but where are the kangaroos and the desert?"

Ellis smiled without taking her eyes off the road. "Most Aussies live in cities. The outback is a long way from here." She checked the mirror twice, the second look lingering on Jacobi. He did not notice. Beretti did.

"Echo Creek sits under Fairwater's station," noted Beretti. "Senior Sergeant Luke Haines is our contact."

"He is," Ellis said, easing them onto a faster road and into arterial streets. "Haines will assist you if he can. Two days ago we had two young women go missing on the Bangera Dam just outside of town. Not sure if it was a drowning or it is related to what you are here for. Haines has been busy organising searches, so you may or may not see him much. I included a brief summary in the folder, given you probably had not heard of that yet with your travels. I will stay this week to get you settled, then head back to Brisbane unless you ask me to stretch."

Jacobi looked over. "What do you think is happening in Echo Creek?"

"Look, I am not here to argue the existence of Yowies. Call it what you like. This town has a problem and I do not think it is human. Eleven missing in five years, three in the last two months. Stories line up from people who do not know each other and do not want their names online. Knocks on walls. Smears on glass higher than any teenager could reach. Yard tools borrowed and put back wrong. Dogs go crazy, then shut up all at once. Howls and screams no one can place. There is a clean run from Devil Monkey Mountain across the winery, through backyards, and under the school fence. Walk it and you get that prickle, like something or someone is watching you."

"You are in an Airbnb on Jensen Street, just off the main strip," Ellis said. "Two bedrooms, decent size, nothing fancy. Lockbox on the rail, code is in your folder. Supermarket one block over, bottle-o next to it, decent coffee on the corner, servo at the highway turn if you want late-night snacks."

"I also have a First Nations contact in town who is willing to help if you need it," she added. "He knows the area and the sites you should respect or avoid. Say the word and I will loop him in."

"Oh, nearly forgot," Ellis said. "A hunter and his mates are in town and heading out at first light. He has been called in to do what other hunters could not. He is known here for causing trouble and not always playing by the rules. You might see him on the main street if you go out for dinner. Name is Cecil Murray. You cannot miss him or his ute. Shock of red hair, about six four, built like a brick house. No filter. Plenty of priors. Drove ten hours to get here. But I can tell you he would not be here without a decent reward on the table. Usually chases feral pigs and deer, but he will put down most anything if he gets enough cash in his pocket."

"Great," Jacobi said. "If he takes down the Yowie tomorrow, our job here is done and we can hit the beach."

Ellis laughed. "If only you were that lucky."

Beretti, ignoring the exchange, turned a page and found a short list with times. "You set interviews."

"Two for tomorrow," Ellis said. "Just waiting on confirmation of times. Morning with Shane at the vineyard; he says he saw something large one night. Then in the arvo we will visit Erin Gowrie, the cousin who wrote to your analyst. I will pick you up in the morning."

City lanes gave up to two-lane blacktop that threaded between cane and pasture, then into a main street with timber verandas and angled parking. A bakery sat busy behind clean glass. A pub leaked low music and fryer smell. Ellis turned left, then right, and put the iX against a weathered cottage painted white with a corrugated roof.

"This is you," she said. "Remember the code is in your folder, keys on a hook just inside. Haines knows you are here and will not drop by unless invited. I will check in after dinner."

Beretti stepped out and glanced up and down the street. Looked like your average small town back home.

They both grabbed their bags out of the SUV and thanked Ellis before she drove off.

Inside, the cottage was tastefully decorated and clean, and looked like it had been thoroughly renovated in the past couple of years. It felt cosy but not stuffy.

Beretti set the folder down, cracked a window for fresh air, and looked to Jacobi, who had already headed down the hallway to secure a bedroom.

CHAPTER 4

Nicole had just set her phone down after sending an update to ASIC Ward when Jacobi called from the bathroom down the hall. "Beretti you need to see this," he said, his voice caught between alarm and a laugh

She walked down the short hall, leaned past him, and looked. The toilet bowl showed water just covering the porcelain. She gave him a light smack on the shoulder with the back of her hand and stepped out before he could see the smile come across her face.

"Apparently it saves water, being so low in the bowl," she said. "You'll survive."

"Cultural immersion begins," he said, grinning as he followed her to the kitchen. "Also, I thought it would be hotter."

"Give it a day; summer can ramp up," she said, setting the folder on the bench and finding the cutlery drawer on the second try.

"Coffee?" he asked.

"Please," she said, studying the machine. After a few minutes of mumbling at buttons while Beretti watched in quiet amusement, he gave up. "Water it is, then."

Beretti kept her mouth shut.

"Hey," Jacobi said, handing her the glass. "You ever chased a Yowie?"

"No," she said. "Came close. An assignment here a few years ago. Cancelled at the last minute."

He absorbed that, then changed lanes. "How are Uncle Ben and Leoni?"

"They enjoyed having us over the holidays," Beretti said, pouring water over two bags. "Ben is busy, as always, and of course Leoni still talks about you. Why she has a soft spot for you I will never know."

Jacobi took a sip of water and gave a small bow. "I washed dishes, went back for thirds, and complimented her coffee.

Hard to beat that value."

"You did put her car in the shop, remember?" Beretti said, chuckling.

"Well, yeah," he said. "That was the deer. She knows that."

Beretti leaned backed in the chair. "By the way, how did Oregon go with your friend?"

"Austin never sits," Jacobi said, a quiet laugh in his voice. "Like he runs on solar and the sun never sets. Rock climbing every second day. ATVs the days between. If a sport works in winter, we did it. Powder, ice, blue mornings. Full of energy, full of life. It was a good run."

"Sounds like it," Beretti replied glancing at the clock. "Five o'clock."

He looked, then checked his phone as if to double-confirm. "What day is it?"

"Wednesday," she said. "Ellis covered that on the drive in."

"Right," he said. "My body will catch up after we eat."

Beretti set her glass in the sink. "Quick shower, then dinner and a walk to get our bearings. How about the pub?"

"Sounds good to me," he said, folding the paper map to the section that mattered."

Jacobi rinsed their cups and sat on the couch reading through his emails. He yawned and wandered what the time was back home but didn't bother checking.

Beretti returned with her hair wrapped in a towel and fresh clothes on.

Jacobi took a quick shower while she dried her hair.

Twenty minutes later, they were ready, locking up and stepping into the cooling evening, ready to eat.

CHAPTER 5

They took the footpath up the main drag with cars drifting past and groups of two and three moving between shops. As they neared the corner pub, Jacobi glanced across the street at a ute that had seen better days, bull bar dented and proud. Wire cages filled the tray. Two dogs watched the footpath with the focused look of dogs who had never felt the comfort of a soft bed.

"I feel sorry for those dogs," he said. "They don't know what they're in for."

"You and me both," Beretti said.

At the door, Jacobi stepped aside and held it for two middle-aged women who beamed at him and offered a cheerful thank you as they went out with takeaway containers balanced in their hands.

Inside smelled like fryers and old timber. A warm guitar line drifted from the speakers under the chatter, something easy and country-rock. Posters ran the walls in no particular order: football heroes shoulder to shoulder with rugby union teams, then a young De Niro, and a fading Monroe. The carpet told long stories. Pool balls cracked.

They found a table near the window and looked over the laminated menu. Burgers, schnitzels, steaks, a long list of sides.

"Burger, fries, side salad," Jacobi said. "I'll try kangaroo while I'm here, but tonight I'll keep it simple. Got to let the gut adjust." He patted his belly.

"Yes, because burger and fries are new to your system," Beretti said, laughing.

He grinned. "Baby steps."

"This place runs a bistro," Beretti said, nodding toward the hatch. "Need to order at the counter."

"I've got it," he said, standing. "What are you having?"

"I'll grab the steak sandwich, thanks."

He came back with a number on a stand and two schooners of the local lager, cold and crisp. The food landed fast. The buns leaned under lettuce, tomato, cheese, a fried egg set right on top, and enough sauce to make a point. Jacobi lifted the lid and laughed under his breath.

"This is not how they build them at home," he said. "Egg on a burger."

"Try it," Beretti said.

He did, then nodded around the second bite. "All right. I'll allow it."

They ate in quiet. Beretti watched the edges of the room while Jacobi tracked the bar, the pool table corner, the heads that turned when the door opened. Busy for a Wednesday. Nothing strange.

When they were done, Jacobi wiped his hands and looked toward the pool tables. "You want to say hi to Cecil Murray and the crew."

"Let's do it," she said.

They crossed the room. Cecil saw them coming and set his cue on the rail. He stood about six foot four, a short orange mohawk, sun-hardened skin, solid through the shoulders under a T-shirt streaked with old smears. His jeans were worn, dust ground in. His gaze ran up and down Beretti without any attempt to hide it. One of his mates gave a wolf whistle for the boys, not at her. She ignored it.

"Let me guess," Cecil said. "You're from the government."

"Not your government," Beretti said.

"Yanks, eh," he said, hearing Beretti's voice up close. He smiled like he was being friendly, eyes not quite matching it. "You're pretty far from home."

"We are where we need to be," Jacobi said, even.

Cecil chuffed a small laugh, glanced at his mates, and spread his hands. "I must be pretty important if you want a yarn with me."

"So, get to it. What do you want with me?" he asked, chalk rolling slow along the tip of his cue.

"We heard you were heading out in the morning," Beretti said. "Chasing something people do not want to talk about. Do you know what you are hunting?"

"I have a fair idea what they reckon is out there, love," he said, shrug in the voice rather than the shoulders. "Forty years in the bush and I will tell you those bloody things do not exist. But if someone is paying, I will take a run. I do not mind being wrong if the fuel gets covered."

One of the men behind him could not help himself. "Tell them about that time down near the border, Cez. When you had a crack at one and…"

Cecil's head turned, smile fixed but eyes hard. "We are talking about tomorrow," he said, soft enough to chill it. The mate shut his mouth.

It was enough for Beretti and Jacobi to clock that he had a point to prove out there.

"Then pack heavy and keep your ears open," Jacobi said. "It is smarter than you think it is."

Cecil held his eye a beat, unreadable and then easy again. "Righto. We will manage, mate."

Cecil tipped his chin at Beretti. "You can come out with us if you like. I will teach you a few things."

"Thanks for the offer," she said. "We will run our own."

He chuckled, low and pleased with himself. "Suit yourself."

Beretti gave a small nod that ended the talk cleanly. They turned for the door.

"Hope I see you again," Cecil called after her with a grin that tried to land somewhere between charm and dare.

Beretti did not turn. "If you're lucky," she said, as they stepped into the evening.

CHAPTER 6

Cecil rolled the ute to a stop at the gate near the base of Devil Monkey Mountain at four in the morning and killed the engine. The sign read NO VEHICLE ACCESS BEYOND THIS POINT. No ranger around at this hour, and he did not want to cop a fine later. The cab already smelled of juniper; Stuey had been at the gin.

They stepped out into the pre-dawn. Cecil shot Stuey a look. "You reek of alcohol. Save it for after."

Stuey grinned and patted the chest pocket of his vest where a small flask rode flat. "Keeps the hands steady."

Cecil clipped him across the cap with the back of his fingers, not hard enough to drop him, hard enough to sting. "It dulls you. Stay sharp or you will put a round through one of us. Get a hold of yourself, mate."

Derick checked his rifle. Warren tightened his pack strap. Alfie, the biggest of the four by a margin, rolled his shoulders once and set his jaw for a long job. He said nothing and stood a touch closer to the group than usual.

Stuey dropped from the tray and set about the dogs: two mixed bully breeds with barrel chests and a steady pull, restless on their feet and ready to turn nose into distance. They had not been fed for two days; Cecil wanted them keen to bite. He stood on the step, took a long look toward Devil Monkey Mountain, and spat dust from the back of his throat.

"This is the spot," he said. "They reckon whatever it is comes off that mountain and runs a corridor behind the vineyard and the houses. If you see anything suss, put it down. And spare me the yowie yarns. Bush is full of pigs and scrubbers, not fairy tales."

Warren snorted. "That government broad is gonna love you, Cecil, when you bring in your whatever-it-is."

Cecil scoffed. "She will, doubt she has ever seen a hunter like me."

Their laughter started. He shut it down with a flat look. "Keep it down, you fucking pelicans."

Stuey clipped the leads long enough to give each dog a nose without a head start. When Cecil slipped them at the old logging cut that drops into the gully corridor, they moved from heel to steam in one run, tails high and mouths open, the track a pale ribbon under pre-dawn grey. The men fell in behind, single file where the scrub pinched and wider where old cuts allowed it. Paperbark and ironbark screened the line, lantana clawed at boots, and dry creek runs glimmered where they would hold water after rain. Barking rose and fell ahead as the pair looped out, their voices keeping the men on line for direction and pace.

"Who told you this is the run," Warren asked, breath steady on the hills.

"Sergeant what's his name," Cecil said. "He says the reports stack the same way."

They walked through dark into a slow, colourless light that pushed along the ridge. When the first edge of day touched the tops, the dogs opened up hard somewhere ahead. Barks stacked fast, snarls tearing at the ends as if they had hit something that pushed back, the sound veering left and driving deeper.

"On," Cecil said, lifting the pace.

The barking rose to a tight wire and then cut. One breath there. The next breath gone.

They stopped together without speaking, the only sound their own lungs catching up. Wind moved high in the canopy. A magpie gave a clipped call and let the morning have the rest. Two sets of footfalls came from the rise to the right, light and fast, and the pair crested a low hill at a dead run and took the track past the men without breaking stride, tongues out and eyes wide, bodies low, driving straight for the gate and the ute.

"What the fuck," Warren said, more annoyed than scared as dust hung low in the corridor the dogs had carved.

"They have never done that before," Derick said. "Not those two."

Cecil swore under his breath. "Ignore the bastards. Keep going."

They walked on into the fresh scratches the dogs had kicked into the earth. The ground offered a short, muddled story: two hurried sets tangled into each other and one angled crossing that did not carry on where it should have. Whatever made that cross kept its weight light on the surface and left little else; the soil here held a shape for a moment and then let it go.

They checked left across the slope and right toward the gully. The quiet felt off. Birds usually got curious when men came through; today the chorus was absent. A wet click kept breaking the silence. After a few steps Cecil placed it: Warren rolling spit along his lips without noticing. In the stillness it carried. "Knock it the fuck off," Cecil said, low. Warren blinked, wiped his mouth. "Right." The sound stopped.

Alfie shifted his grip on the rifle and let his other hand rest on the strap near his chest, a small tell he did not seem to notice.

"Still reckon pigs," Stuey said, lower now.

"Could be," Cecil said, words flat. "Could be a scrubber bull. Could be you lot are jumping at nothing. Eyes up. Do not stare at your boots. The ground is not going to wave at you."

They worked the flank along the corridor toward the vineyard's back fence where rows stepped neat down to the gully. At a choke point where bank met wire, prints held in the damp silt laid by last night's dew. Not boots and not roo. Wider than a man's heel and longer, toes softened by the give in the earth.

"Kids with boards," Cecil said, already shaking his head.

"Seen it. Blokes with time and nothing to do."

"Boards leave edges," Derick said, crouching in. "This does not."

"And pigs do not set toes like that," Warren added. "Not cloven."

Alfie bent at the knees rather than the waist and took a longer look, then straightened and studied the fence line toward the houses. "How far to the school from here," he asked, casual on the surface. His eyes kept flicking to the margins.

"A kilometre or more," Cecil said. "Could be a weird wash. Could be backfill slumped on a dog print. Do not build a story off one mark."

On a split twig near chest height, a dark smear gave off a sour note like the bottom of an old tank. Stuey leaned in, nostrils pulling, then stepped back.

"That is not mud," he said. "And it bloody stinks."

He turned his back to the others and took another swallow. Cecil reached out and cuffed him again, sharper this time, a flat crack of palm to cap.

"Last warning," Cecil said. "You want to drink, do it when I am not responsible for your decisions."

"Righto," Stuey mumbled.

"Still want us to shoot anything unusual," Warren asked, not trying for a joke.

"If it fronts up," Cecil said. "If it hangs back, we make sure before we shoot. I am not walking into town with a dead farmhand and an apology. And I am not dropping some clown in a ghillie suit because the bush made you jump."

They pushed another hundred metres until the corridor opened on a patch where flood had once laid the silt smooth. Something heavy had crossed recently. Long stride. Clean weight. No tail drag. No cloven line. Alfie's breath came a little shorter for a few steps and then levelled. He slid half a pace closer to the others without making a thing of it.

Derick looked over. "Tell me that is kids with boards."

"Tell me it is not," Warren said, eyes on the spacing.

Cecil's mouth went dry and he blamed the lack of water, not the shapes at his feet. Irritation stiffened his voice. "We take the fence toward the school, then cut back up to the ridge. And if I smell that flask again before the gate, I will pour it on your boots, Stuey."

Stuey lifted a palm. "Got it."

They set off along the gully edge with the mountain behind them and a town ahead that would wake soon to coffee and school bells. The morning said nothing. Cecil kept to his usual caution; it had served him for decades. The others left room for being wrong. Alfie kept his eyes moving and his place a fraction nearer the middle than usual. None of them voiced any of it. The corridor offered no opinion.

CHAPTER 7

Belinda woke to light on the wall, two pale ovals sliding across the ceiling and settling over the curtains. Headlights. Jared's shift always ran late on a Thursday morning. She smiled at the thought he was home. They had been married six months and were still learning each other's rhythms. They had moved inland from Bundaberg for his job, and she worked admin at the school. She turned her face into the pillow and let sleep take her again.

When she woke again the room was quiet and still bright. The glow hadn't moved. The lamp on Jared's side was dark, and the sheet there held only the weight she had left on it when she rolled. She reached for her phone on the bedside table and paused when a key found the front door. Metal on metal, a small turn she knew by heart. Out front, the headlights shut off on their own.

Jared came down the hall and stepped straight to the window. He drew the curtain closed with two careful fingers, held it there a second as if testing the fabric, then sat on the end of the bed. The mattress dipped and stayed that way. She pushed up on one elbow.

"What's wrong?"

He didn't answer. He fixed his eyes on a point above the dresser and held himself still. His hands hung between his knees.

"Jared."

He turned his head enough for her to see his face. The color had left it. His gaze slipped past her shoulder toward the window again before coming back.

"When I pulled in," he said, voice thin and flat, "something was crouched in the tree by our window. Big. Too big for a person to be up there like that. Hell, I don't even know how the limbs didn't break."

Belinda's hand found the edge of the doona and held it. "In the tree," she said, quiet to keep the words from shaking.

"It was there," he said. "Head turned toward the glass. When the lights hit it, it dropped. It didn't turn towards me, so I never saw its face. Hit the ground soft and went. Not a scramble and not a climb. Just down and gone. Faster than any bloke can move. Faster than anything should move."

He swallowed and looked at his hands as if he had only just noticed the tremor. "I sat in the truck for half an hour. Watched the mirrors. Waited to see if it came back. I thought I was gonna pass out my heart was beating so fast."

"So it was looking in," Belinda said. The thought settled in her chest and would not move.

He lifted his chin a fraction and met her eyes for the first time. "Yes."

"What was it."

"I don't know." He shook his head once. "I had the beams on it for a second, maybe less. Hair all over. Big across the shoulders. Long. Not a roo. Not a person. I know both in a light. It wasn't either."

Her skin prickled from scalp to heel. She swung her legs out of bed and pulled on his hoodie from the chair, the fabric holding a faint mix of detergent, Jared, and truck cab. He reached out a hand, not quite blocking her.

"Don't go outside," he said. "Not unless I'm with you. Not even for the bin. Not this week."

"I'm not stepping out there," she said, and meant it.

They sat with the space between them full of the thing she had not seen. She could tell how hard he worked to keep his breath even. He rubbed his thumbs together and then made himself stop. She watched him stand, cross to the window again, and lift the curtain a finger's width. It barely moved.

"Leave it," she said.

"I'm only looking at the yard," he said. "The fence line."

"Is it gone?"

"I fucking hope so," he said. He let the fabric fall back into place and returned to the bed.

He told her the shape again, stripping it down to details. Where it held itself on the branch. The way the glare had washed out any shine from the eyes so he was left with outline and weight that felt wrong in his head. The jump. The speed once it hit ground. He didn't know if he could trust his own eyes.

"You're not to go outside alone," he said, finishing where he had started. "We lock up for real tonight. Bathroom window. Laundry door. Everything."

"I know," she said. "Get some sleep. After that, we call the police."

He nodded, the decision landing without argument.

He walked the house before he tried lying down. She heard deadbolts slide and the soft thud of his palm testing frames. While he made the circuit, she went to the kitchen, warmed milk in a small pot, and brought it back in a mug that kept her hands busy.

"You think it was something paranormal?" she asked, keeping her voice low.

"No. No. It looked real. Not see-through, not a trick of light. I heard its feet hit the ground over the engine. It was a soft thud yet sounded heavy. Whatever it is, it belongs to this world."

She let that settle and watched him drink, slow and careful.

They lay down without turning off the lamp. She felt him stay high on the mattress, not sinking into sleep, body angled so he could hear the hall and the yard at once. She tried to line her thoughts up and could not. The image she had built from his words kept shifting. A weight in the tree. A posture that made no sense for a person. The glass two steps from her feet and the knowledge that something had been there with its attention turned inward.

"Maybe it was passing through," she said, hating how small that sounded.

"Maybe," he said. "It chose our tree, though."

She did not answer that. She watched the lamp throw a soft circle over the wardrobe and the chair and the hoodie she had not taken off. The room had not changed. Her eyes had.

When her pulse settled enough to let her breathe without counting, she drifted close to sleep and jerked awake to the sound of nothing. The clock in the kitchen kept up its tick. A car went by on the road and faded. Somewhere a fridge motor kicked in and then out. Everything ordinary lay over the top of what had just happened and did nothing to lighten it.

Jared did not sleep. She felt it in the way he sat up every few minutes and listened without checking the window. When he finally slid down and let his head find the pillow, dawn had begun to touch the skirting with a grey that made the lamp unnecessary.

Belinda turned the switch with two fingers and the room dropped to that early light. Through a narrow line in the curtain she could see the tree. One branch hung heavier than it had yesterday. Bark looked roughed on the side that faced the house.

She felt Jared watching her profile.

"Stay inside," he said, before she could speak it. "Today and tonight."

She nodded and laid her head back on the pillow.

CHAPTER 8

The hunters followed the fence toward the school until the vines broke into scrub and a gully that tightened like a throat. The dogs were gone in the direction of the ute. Cecil called that a blessing because they were noisy and prone to chasing the wrong thing. No one argued. A sour, damp note rode low under the paperbarks. A thin bar of dawn touched the ridge, but under the canopy it stayed mostly dark.

"Pick it up," Cecil said, heel pressing into silt that held a print for a breath. "We cut to the ridge after the next bend."

Alfie edged closer to the centre without making a show of it. Derick split his sight between ground and distance. Warren scanned the backs of the yards whenever fences appeared beyond the gully. Stuey took a short pull, wiped his mouth, and tucked the flask when Cecil's head turned.

Something altered up ahead. Not a clean sighting. A darker seam tucked into trunk and shadow that had not been there, then was, then wasn't. They stopped together.

"You saw that?" Warren said, voice already tight.

"No," Cecil said. "And neither did you. Move."

They did. Ten paces. Fifteen. A stone clicked near Alfie's boot, rolled once, and settled against his laces. Not thrown hard. Placed from further than any man should place anything.

"Fucking kids," Cecil said, flat. "Or a farmer with a death wish. Stay tight."

They reached a choke where bank and fence pressed close and shoulders met bark. The sour note thickened until it lived on tongues. Derick pointed at a smear on wire and kept his hands off it. The skin on top had dried yet still looked new, which made no sense.

"Leave it," Cecil said.

A single heavy step landed behind them. Not close and not far. Enough weight to drum in ribs. Derick spun. Trees.

Silt. Their own tracks. Nothing that should make a step like that.

"Cecil," Alfie said. "This spot is wrong."

"Stop your whining," Cecil said.

They slid through the squeeze and into a pocket where the gully widened a fraction. A heavy stank rolled through the air. Stuey's breath came loud. Derick hissed to hush and something large came in low from the right, soundless until it was almost on them.

Cecil turned. Trunk and shadow resolved into height and width that mocked sense. It took him by the shirt and belt together and dragged him into tea-tree with speed that left no room for shouting. Branches cracked. Pale trunks flexed. A shape moved and was gone. No face. No hands. Just mass and motion and a man erased.

Derick brought the rifle up, held fire because any shot risked Cecil, and the scrub answered with a chest-deep blast of air that struck nerves and raised skin.

"Cecil," Warren called, panic scraping the name. The bush gave him nothing back.

Stuey lurched toward the sound, bravado and gin trying

to hold his spine. "Who the fuck is there?" he barked. He swept the muzzle in sharp arcs, hacking at cover that refused to be cut. A long limb came from the green and hit him across the ribs. The blow lifted him and dumped him sideways. He wheezed, pushed to his knees, then staggered upright with a hand to his side. "Fucking asshole. Show yourself," he snapped, voice shaking.

Derick fired once, a warning into the green. Wood jumped. Leaf shredded. A deep, menacing growl came from the dark. The thing shifted a fraction. Not hurt. Annoyed. "Back," Warren said, stumbling. "Back, back."

"H e e e e l p," Cecil yelled, long and wet, the word dragged until it sounded like his throat would tear. It carried for a full second, then a brutal crack and a heavy thud cut it short, loud and close, a sound with the weight of bones breaking.

Silence fell hard.

"Run," Derick snapped. He could not steady the muzzle. He sucked air that tasted of rot and tank water. "Move."

They came apart and then forced themselves into a unit again. The scrub swelled around their shins as if the ground wanted them slow. Alfie drove his shoulder into Warren to shove him along the slit between bank and fence. Derick backed them, rifle up and useless against cover this thick. Stuey limped, teeth bared, one arm wrapped over his ribs.

Another stone tapped behind Derick's heel. A second pebble kissed dust in front of Warren's knee.

They ran.

The pocket broke into a flood-run. Silt slid under boots. Warren glanced back once and wished he had not; a dark silhouette ran the bank above them and paced without sound, a suggestion more than a sight, fast as running water.

"Go, go!" Derick yelled. "Through the fence."

They hit the barbed wire together and spread along four spots on the same run. Warren shoved his shoulder under the top strand while Derick hauled up on it, metal singing and teeth biting into his palms. Alfie flattened a section with his boot and slid sideways through, jacket ripping and skin scratched raw. Warren kicked and spilled through on the far side. Derick twisted, scraped free with a grunt, and stumbled after him.

Stuey did not clear. His belt snagged and a heel wedged. He yanked and the wire bit deeper. "Help me!" he yelled, desperate. The fence shivered. Something moved in the dark behind them. Stuey clawed for dirt and leaves, breath breaking, the strand pinning him at the hips. A quick jerk caught his ankle and dragged him backward. The wire scored skin, fabric tore, and the sound that left his throat did not belong to courage.

Derick dropped to a knee and fired into the dark at muzzle's length. The flash blew bark and spat splinters into his cheek. The drag on Stuey slackened for a blink and then came back twice as hard. Nails peeled. A heel popped from the boot with a wet sound. "No. No." Stuey babbled, voice gone thin and small.

Warren grabbed a sleeve. The seam exploded in his fist. Stuey slid another half metre into scrub and screamed high and wild.

Alfie stood with his hands on his head, a look of helplessness fixed on his face.

Derick fired again, lower. Silt turned to mist. The answer rolled out of the tea-tree as a single deep note that shivered wire and leaf. Stuey's scream stretched to a string and then snapped. Something inside him cracked loud. The thud that followed had finality.

Alfie stared at the gap, hoping Stuey might somehow come back out. Warren shoved him. 'Run, dammit,' he snarled.

They ran. The gully bent left and the corridor loosened. Scrub gave to old cut. Old cut gave to gravel. Gravel hammered their soles and spit under the tray as they reached the compacted apron near the gate. The ute sat where they had left it, nose pointed to the road. The dogs were already in their cages, pressed to mesh, eyes fixed forward, mouths shut as if silence could make them smaller.

One latch hung open. Warren slapped it down and jammed the pin. It missed the hole, skittered off, and rang the tray. He swore, lined it again, and drove it home with a palm that left a bloody crescent.

"Keys," he said, breath torn into pieces.

"Tyre," Derick said. "Front left."

Warren dropped to a knee, reached up behind the guard, and felt grit, then tape, then cold metal. He ripped the spare key free from where Cecil always hid it on the tyre, shoved it into Derick's hand, and sprinted for the passenger door.

Derick threw the rifle into the tray and clawed the driver's handle. The key slid once, then turned. The engine coughed. For a heartbeat it hesitated, a dead thing asking for mercy. Then it caught and shook itself awake.

Alfie tumbled into the back seat and yanked the door in with his heel. Warren hit the passenger seat and braced both hands on the dash. A stone hit the quarter panel with a dull thunk and skittered off into the weeds.

Derick dropped the clutch too fast and the ute hopped, then bit. They shot down the trail and onto the bitumen. Tyres spat gravel that rattled on guards and fell away. Warren glanced once into the mirror and saw nothing he could use, only trees that kept their own secrets and a mouth of scrub that closed as if it had never opened.

Something moved in the timber to the right. It ran the verge for three beats, a long dark line that showed no detail, then peeled back into the tea-tree without a sound. Derick felt the hair lift on his forearms and did not speak. He pushed his foot harder to the floor. The needle climbed. Wind climbed with it and forced the last of the stink out of the cab.

They hit the first bend too quick. The ute squirmed on the loose and came straight when Derick gave it a calm hand. The cages thudded and then settled. The dogs did not make a sound. Alfie pressed a rag to his ear and held it until the blood stopped flowing down his jaw. Warren stared straight ahead and tried not to hear bones in the engine note.

Derick kept the ute pointed at town and let the speed do

work. They did not speak. They did not turn the radio on. Wind filled the cab, and the mountain fell away behind them until it was only a line over the dogs' cages and a memory laid across their shoulders.

CHAPTER 9

Jacobi spread the map on the kitchen table, two empty mugs waiting. The rental's coffee machine was fussy enough to need its manual; Beretti wrestled with it, learned the sequence, and won. She set the coffees down and took the seat opposite. The room filled with fresh roast warmth. She traced the town grid until her finger found the gully again, the line locals had drawn with stories and worry, while Jacobi went over the witness list and tapped two names that kept turning up across statements.

A knock carried through the front door, three even raps. Jacobi stood, wiped his hands on his jeans, and opened up to a man in blue police uniform on the step: short sleeves with patches and nameplate, duty belt set for a long day, boots salted with dust. Mid-forties, lean and long in the frame, sun-browned, crow's-feet cut deep at the corners of steady eyes, hair clipped close enough to pass for a buzz if you didn't look twice. He removed his cap.

"Sergeant Craig Hofner, Echo Creek Police," he said, offering a hand to Jacobi and then to Beretti as she stepped into view. "Ms Beretti. Mr Jacobi."

"Sergeant," Beretti said. "Come in."

He entered and paused in the kitchen doorway, professional and ready to move. "Senior Sergeant Haines can't step away. He's on scene. We had an incident this morning."

"The hunters," Beretti said.

"Yes. Two men missing," Hofner answered, taking in the open file and the map without slowing. "They were walking the gully before sunup. We need to move."

"Can you drive us?" Beretti asked, already closing the file and sliding it into her satchel. "We don't have a rental, yet."

"Sure. I'll take you," he said. "Less chance of losing you in back streets."

They grabbed their go-bags and their gun bags and

locked up.

Out on the small front landing the street lay quiet in the hour before school and work. A marked Hilux idled at the curb. A metallic blue SUV rolled across the driveway with a soft electric whirr and settled; Taylor Ellis stepped out with a zing in her step, AFP crest at the shoulder, hair swept back, face set to the job and eyes already taking stock.

"Morning," she said. Her glance landed on Jacobi first. "I've got the update. Ready to roll?" She gave Beretti a quick nod. "We'll link at the scene."

"Ride with me, Jacobi," Ellis added. "Hofner will lead."

"All right," Jacobi said.

"Any media yet," Beretti asked Hofner as they moved.

"A caller tipped the pub, and the texts are going around," he said. "We've told people to stay clear. That will last about five minutes."

"Then let's move," Beretti said.

They loaded fast. Jacobi tossed his bag into the BMW's back seat and buckled in. Ellis drove like someone who knew every dip and camber and kept both hands settled on the wheel while Hofner pulled away first and let them fall in behind. On a broad stretch of road a field opened to the left; a mob of kangaroos froze among low scrub with ears twitching, then bounded together toward a fenceline, and Jacobi watched them go with a quiet smile he kept to himself as the highway curved.

"Two missing," Ellis said as the town slipped behind them. "Cecil and Stuey. The three who made it out are Derick, Warren and Alfie. I spoke to them briefly at the station. They were rattled, alright." She checked her mirror and returned to the flow.

"Don't blame them," Jacobi said.

Eliss waited a beat then glanced to her left.

"You two been partners long?"

"About eight months now, I think," Jacobi said. "She's got the brain and I like to think I've got the brawn but in reality, she would kick my ass any day." He gave a small shrug.

"Sounds like a good partner," Ellis said, the corner of her mouth tipping. "Family back home?"

"Yeah," he said. "Haven't spoken to them in years. Best that way."

"Jet lag treating you all right?"

"I'll be human by tomorrow," he said. "Kangaroos helped."

She laughed under her breath. "We can arrange more of those. What do you do when you're not working?"

"Climb when I can. Bad guitar. Good coffee. I visit friends who try to break me with activity." He thought of Oregon and shook his head, still amused. "One of them has a talent for making weekends feel like boot camp."

"Well, it keeps you fit," Ellis said, glancing over at him before turning back to the road.

"What about you?" Jacobi asked.

"My life is about my work," Ellis said after a moment. "Family in Adelaide. I catch up with them on holidays. Other than that, nobody."

"If you need anything while you're here, you tell me first," she added, tone cool and professional but warmer at the edges.

"Appreciate it," Jacobi said, missing the layer she had laid under the words.

Hofner turned toward Devil Monkey Mountain, angling for the base. The town receded, and low hills shouldered up on either side. His indicator blinked left to a dirt spur that ran along the treeline and ended at a maintenance gate ribboned with blue-and-white tape. Beyond it the verge held two marked units, a scenes van with doors open, and another SUV with kits laid out; uniforms worked the line while white-suited techs moved careful under the trees.

They braked in behind the tape. Gravel ticked under tyres as the engines settled. Hofner climbed out and set his cap. Waiting at the line was a stocky man in stripes, about six feet, shoulders square, close-cropped hair silvering at the temples, forearms thick from years of work. No nonsense in his stance, eyes steady and direct. When he spoke, his voice sat deep and carried without effort.

"Senior Sergeant Luke Haines," he said, shaking once with each of them, grip firm without show, attention already pulling back to the scrub. "Thanks for getting here quickly." He pointed with a gloved hand down the corridor of tea-tree and paperbark. "We've got one confirmed, Cecil Murray. He's a way in and in very bad shape. Looks like he was thrown against a tree. Neck's snapped. We're still looking for the other one."

"Any tracks?" Jacobi asked.

"Here and there," Haines said. "With this dry ground, not much sticks."

They followed the narrow dirt track for a time, eyes down for sign. Whatever could be read had been lifted or muddied by police and scene techs. Beretti let her gaze run the gully. A sour taint rode low in the air and clung to cloth.

Haines lifted the tape and stepped aside. "Stay on the flagged path. Do not touch the fence until forensics signs off. Derick, Warren, and Alfie are at the station now. Beretti, Jacobi, you're welcome to interview them whenever you're ready."

Beretti's focus came on clean as she ducked under the tape. The ground changed from the grit of the rows to damp silt that didn't hold prints. Jacobi and Ellis came in behind her, observing, and Hofner took the rear.

They reached a sagging run of barbed wire. Blood spotted the grass at its base. The earth was kicked and gouged. There had been a scuffle. Drag marks led off into the scrub.

"This matches what the three men told us," Haines said. "Stuey was dragged off the fence. The others bolted for the ute. Scene techs photographed and took samples."

He pointed along the flagged line. "We followed the drag

marks but haven't found a body yet. I've got officers scanning the scrub now. Next scene is down here."

They carried on until two techs and a uniform rose into view a few metres off the track, holding a small perimeter in the trees. What remained of Cecil lay there.

"Let's see the body," Beretti said.

Cecil was racked into a paperbark trunk, one leg folded under at the wrong angle. His head sat canted and too loose on the neck. Shirt torn. Ribs on one side had pushed skin into a strange swell. Bark pressed into his cheek. Smaller chips fanned where the hit had shaken the tree.

A tech measured from the trunk to an arc of scuffs in leaf litter.

"How far?" Jacobi asked.

"Four and a bit," the tech said.

"Thrown," Jacobi told Beretti.

Beretti moved to the clear side and studied the trunk. Long rakes where something had driven Cecil in.

A tech crouched near a knee-high sapling and held up two brass casings in a glove. "Two spent," he said. ".308 by the base. Ten metres back from the trunk."

"Derick fired into the bush," Haines said, stepping to a shallow depression with a scuff where a toe had dug in. "Lines up."

Another tech eased a ladder against the paperbark while a partner plucked a small tuft from a tear two metres up and slid it into a vial.

"Height," Jacobi said, looking up. "If that smear came from the subject, it's tall, or momentum lifted it."

Ellis drifted in from the perimeter. "Big enough to pick up a man by shirt and belt," she said.

Hofner crouched at Cecil's left hand and checked the nails. "No cuts," he said. "He didn't get his hands up."

"Came in fast," Haines said. "Grabbed. Threw. No time for anything else."

"Any prints that aren't boots?" Jacobi asked.

"Depressions," a tech said. "Too much leaf for ridges. Weight near that rub, like something stood and shifted."

After a few minutes, they headed back the way they'd come.

"You think Stuey's still alive?" Ellis asked, looking down the trail.

Jacobi took a moment. "They rarely keep people alive. It might have moved him for later."

Haines's jaw set. "My team will keep looking. We're already stretched searching for those two girls."

"Any luck so far?" Beretti asked.

"No, unfortunately. It's like they disappeared into thin air," Haines said. "Their families are beside themselves."

They continued back down the trail, passing techs and more searchers pushing into the scrub.

Back at the cars, Beretti said, "It's likely bunkered down now for daylight."

Haines nodded. "Agreed."

Ellis looked toward the road. "Jacobi and Beretti can ride with me to the station, then we'll carry on with our initial plans to interview past witnesses."

Haines's radio cracked. He listened, keyed once, then clipped it back. "Dispatch reports an incident at a home last night on the outskirts," he said. "Might be related. No injuries reported. I'll head back to the station and get the details. I'll send you the address."

"Thanks," Beretti said. "If it lines up, we'll swing past after the station."

Ellis unlocked the BMW. Jacobi sat in the back, Beretti in the passenger seat. The air still carried that low sour note that came out of the trees and clung to cloth.

CHAPTER 10

The police station had that early-morning buzz and everyone looked and felt fresh. Haines met them at the front desk, gave a quick nod toward Interview Two, and let them settle. The room was square and plain, with a recorder in the middle and a jug of water that tasted like pipes.

Derick came in with a constable, hat in both hands, the ordeal looking like it had added ten years to his face. Warren and Alfie followed, Warren looking all around, nervous and jittery, Alfie quiet and closed in, each of them marked with open cuts on their faces and arms, the palms of their hands split with dried blood.

Haines gave a quick intro and stepped back to the wall. Ellis read the time onto the recorder, kept her voice even, and had each man state his name and affirm that what he was about to say was the truth, then asked Derick to start from the beginning.

"Yeah, right," Derick said, rubbing a thumb along the hat brim. "We parked up about four. The dogs started carrying on, then shot back to the ute on their own. We pushed into the gully, hit that tight bit at the fence, and I heard a step behind us, heavy, not like a bloke. Next breath, Cecil was gone. It grabbed his shirt and belt and dragged him into the scrub so quick I didn't get a proper look. I fired into the bush. We ran for the fence. Derick met their eyes in turn. "The three of us made it through." He paused, breath catching. "Alfie, the poor bugger, got hung on the barbs. Something grabbed his boot and hauled him back under. I tried to hold onto him."

"Where were the keys?" Beretti asked.

"On the tyre," he said. "Warren grabbed them. I drove. My hands were already on the wheel by the time we slammed the doors."

"Cecil," Ellis said, softer. "When did you hear him last?"

Derick's eyes fell to the table. "He yelled for help, long and a bit wet at the end," he said. "Then it sounded like something cracked and hit, real heavy."

Warren cleared his throat and leaned forward, elbows on knees. "What he said's right." He shook his head, eyes on the floor. "Should've listened to the bloody dogs. They knew something was up."

"Did any of you notice a smell?" Jacobi asked.

Warren nodded. "Yeah. Like wet dog and faeces. And that sour tank stink when water sits."

Beretti tapped her pen once. "Did any of you get a look at it? Not a guess. A look."

The three men glanced at each other and shook their heads.

"No," Alfie said. "Just shadows. Big. Bloody big." He paused. "What's funny is, Cecil never believed in yowies, but if it was anything, I'd bet my life it was one."

Beretti slid the water their way and let them drink. "You got out when most wouldn't," she said, steady rather than kind.

They nodded. Ellis clicked the recorder off, signed the forms, and left copies with them. Haines said he would run them home after a medic checked them over.

****

Ellis had the address up on her phone before they hit the car park. "Alrighty. Western edge of town," she said as they climbed into the BMW. "Jared and Belinda. He finished a late shift and pulled in with headlights straight at the bedroom window. Saw something large and then it took off."

"Same one or another?" Jacobi said, buckling in.

"One until its proven otherwise," Beretti said. "We still plan like two is possible."

They took the two-lane out past the last paddocks. The house sat behind a windbreak of gums and a low fence, with a white company ute tucked under a carport. Belinda opened the door, hair pulled back, eyes tired but sharp, and brought them into a neat room that felt lived in. Jared stood by the window, unsure of what to do with his hands.

Ellis showed ID, asked to record, and set her phone on the table. "Can you run us through last night," she said, easy and clear. "Start from when you got home."

"Just before four," Jared said, eyes still on the yard. "We clocked off about twenty past three. I grabbed a pie at the servo and drove straight home, twenty minutes or so. As I turned into the driveway something looked wrong. Like out of place."

"In the tree," Jacobi said, keeping it open.

"Yeah. Something crouched along the limb," Jared said, hand flattening against the glass without thinking. "Back to me. Too big to be anyone I know. Lights hit it and it dropped, then it ran. I didn't see a face, just back and legs, and it covered ground way too quick. Never seen something move that freakin fast."

"How long did you stay in the ute," Beretti asked.

"About half an hour," he said. "I kept waiting to see if it came back. When I couldn't sit there any longer I came in."

Belinda took the thread, voice steady. "I woke up when the headlights were on the wall and smiled because I thought he was home, then drifted off again. I woke up later and the bed was empty. I was just about to call Jared when I heard the key in the door. He went straight to the window and pulled the curtain, and he sat on the end of the bed and looked like he had seen a ghost. I told him to check the doors and windows, made him a warm milk because that is what my nan always did, and he told me not to go outside without him.

He said it looked real, not see-through, and he could hear the foot hits over the engine."

"Did you move anything outside this morning," Ellis asked. "Clean up prints or sweep the porch."

"No," Belinda said. "We left it."

Jacobi stepped out with Jared and walked the line of the headlights to the window. The limb was solid, though the scuffs in the bark sat higher than his reach. The soil under the window was thin, but a deep toe dig had held, and two small stones had rolled out of the mulch near the fence like something had dropped hard, planted, and pushed off.

"You heard it jump?" Jacobi said.

"Over the engine," Jared said. "This thing had bulk but it was all in the shoulders. Skinny waist from what I could see."

Jared shifted and looked at the ground and then back up at Jacobi. "I know how it sounds," he said. "I'm not trying to be that bloke, but I know what I saw and heard."

Jacobi met his eyes. "I believe you, man."

Inside, Ellis said they would have a patrol roll past after dark. Belinda thanked her and asked if they should stay with family.

"If it makes you feel better, do it," Ellis said. "If you stay, keep doors and windows shut and try to light the yard up as best as they can."

They stepped back onto the porch. The windbreak carried bird noise and the sun was edging to midday. Beretti looked over her notes and drew the line that mattered.

"He pulls in just before 4a.m.," she said. "The hunters were at the gate at four and reached the pinch around four twenty. That puts this house first, it takes off and comes across the five men."

"Or we are dealing with two," Jacobi replied.

"Maybe," Beretti replied. "But my gut says only one."

"Well, it is usually right," Jacobi added. He gave the limb one last look, took in the scuffed bark sitting higher than any easy reach and the toe dig that did not read like a boot, and closed the door.

"Can we check out the dam next?" Beretti asked, glancing at Ellis.

"Sure," Ellis said, reversing and turning onto the main road.

CHAPTER 11

Ellis turned off the road onto the narrow strip of bitumen that hugs the reservoir and parked beside the single concrete ramp. Across the dam at the maintenance entrance, a few police and SES vehicles sat nose-to-rail. Bangera was ringed by heavy brush and tall timber, the shoreline broken into shelves of gravel, dirt and rock. There was one launch for small craft, a tin pontoon with grey boards, and a couple of picnic tables pulled back under the gums. No one else was around.

Ellis watched as Beretti and Jacobi hopped out, slung their go-bags, and unzipped a separate weapons case. Their sidearms were already on their hips; they lifted out two rifles.

"You think you'll need those?" she asked.

"We never take the chance," Jacobi said, looking up briefly.

Ellis tapped the pistol on her hip. "Okay," she said quietly.

They took the path along the western arm. Ellis kept her eyes on the ground and laid out the case while they walked.

"Maddie and Jamie," she said. "Both twenty-two. Best friends since primary school. They came here most afternoons, so nothing about that day looked out of character. They just didn't make it home. The family came looking and found the tinny drifting in this arm. Police ran a quick search that night and came back at first light. No sign of the girls. Their phones were gone and there was no signal off them. Shoes missing from the boat, a couple of clothes missing, and not much else to go on."

"Did anyone see them in the boat? Looks like a popular picnic spot," Jacobi asked.

"Not that I've heard," Ellis said.

They stopped where the family had first seen the tinny drifting. A rock at the waterline held a fresh scrape, silver against old paint. On the dirt above it, searcher prints had churned the fine detail flat. A thread caught on a twig hung like a stray fishing line hair. Beretti took a photo and moved on.

"Plenty of feet after," Jacobi said, taking in the trampled patch.

"We will not get clean first sign here," Beretti said. "We can still build shape."

They worked the bank. Reeds ticked together. An old fire ring sat cold. Names carved in a flat rock carried dates and hearts. Nothing useful until the ground dipped into a shallow ramp that made an easy path out of the water. Shade had kept a little moisture and the impressions held.

"Large impression," Jacobi said, crouching without touching. "Edges are smeared… could be a double step."

"Close together," Beretti said. "Could be something. Could be someone who came through with the search."

Ellis photographed the spot and marked it on her phone.

They reached the spillway road, a cracked strip of concrete chained off between two posts. Above it the embankment rose in a slope of dirt and rock with scrub clinging where it could. The opposite shore sat across a stretch of water that looked shorter than it was.

They stood a moment and let the place settle. Far out, a line of ripples ran straight and faded. A swallow dipped under the pontoon and did not show again.

"Anyone else feel like we are being watched?" Jacobi

asked, voice even.

"Yes," Beretti said. She tipped her chin at the rise above the chain. "From the embankment."

"I feel it too," Ellis said, keeping her gaze steady.

"Let's keep moving," Jacobi said. "Eyes and ears open."

They climbed beside the chain and stepped onto the old road. Up on the embankment, loose rock slid a little underfoot. From here the water lay open. From below, anyone sitting up here would be hard to spot unless they stood. A dust film on a flat rock showed a tight crescent where a heel had pivoted. A small heap of gravel had slumped in a way that looked like a kick, not wash. A branch at shoulder height had snapped recently, leaves still green. A patch of grass in the shade lay pressed flat where someone had sat long enough to leave a shape.

"People come up here," Ellis said quietly. "But this place feels... wrong."

They dropped off the far side, took a narrow track along the slope, and came out above a pocket of shore where people park to throw a line. The edge told a small story. Toes dug in and heels turned. A ring in the wet silt where something heavy had rested. Two faint drag lines that ran for a metre and disappeared on rock.

They followed the curve until the launch came into view again. The sense of eyes on them stayed like a pressure change, never sharp enough to point at, never gone. None of them said anything more about it.

Ellis angled toward a weatherboard cottage near the entry road, a rain tank tucked close and a ute under a carport. The gate sign read PRIVATE RESIDENCE. A kelpie on the veranda watched them, head on paws. Doug Glass, Bangera Dam's caretaker and site overseer, opened the door before they could knock, boots dusted red, work shirt clean at the collar, a neat grey beard on a sun-cut face. Introductions were quick and the kettle went on. They kept it polite and practical, saved the harder questions for a second pass, and didn't stay long.

"Pleasant enough, but nothing new," Beretti said. "He didn't see the girls that day."

"Agreed," Ellis said. "Worth a shot."

When they stepped back into the light and headed for the BMW, all three stopped at once. Sitting in the middle of Ellis's bonnet was a girl's white canvas sneaker. It was clean. It was dry. The laces had been tucked down inside.

Ellis went still. "Clearly, that was not here when we

parked."

"No," Beretti said. She scanned the verge, then the tree line, then the water. "Gloves."

Jacobi swept the embankment with a slow, careful look. "Nothing moving," he said. "I'll keep an eye out while you check the shoe."

Beretti pulled nitriles from her bag, took photos from three angles, and lifted the shoe off the paint. Women's size six. No obvious mud. A worn brand stamp and a partial number on the tongue.

Ellis opened the boot so Beretti could bag it. Her voice stayed low. "If this is a joke, it is a sick one."

"It is not a joke," Beretti said. She sealed the bag and met her eyes. "Something or someone placed it on your car."

They stood with the BMW between them and the water, that watching feeling back at the edge of thought. The trees kept their secrets. The dam lay still. Somewhere a dog barked twice and stopped.

"Alright, let's get out of here," Beretti said.

CHAPTER 12

As they entered town, Ellis glanced over from the driver's seat. "You two hungry?"

"Always," Jacobi said.

"Good. You're in for a real Aussie treat." She pulled up outside a corner bakery with a chalkboard menu and the smell of butter and gravy drifting out the door.

At the case, Beretti pointed to a steak pie. Jacobi tapped the glass at steak and pepper, then added mince and cheese, eyes wide at all the options. Ellis went chicken and veg and paid before they could argue, and they each grabbed a soft drink from the fridge.

They took a window table. Steam rolled up as Jacobi

cracked his first pie. "These are worth sitting on a plane for sixteen hours."

"Told you," Ellis said. "Quick Aussie 101 while you eat. Servo is a service station. Arvo is afternoon. Rego is registration. Bottle-o is the liquor store. Smoko is a smoke break. Ambos are paramedics. Garbo is the bin truck driver. If we can slap an 'o' on it, we will."

Beretti smiled. "Noted. I am sure Jacobi will remember all of them in no-time."

Jacobi lifted the mince and cheese next. "I think I'm in love."

Both women laughed as Jacobi downed the pie in seconds.

"Aright. Next stop, Erin's place, the one who kicked this off," Ellis said as she pushed her chair in.

At Jacobi's insistence, they boxed a second round for later and headed out.

****

A little after three they turned off the bitumen and into a narrow drive between low gums. It opened on a weathered cottage set square to the gully. Six acres stretched behind it, mostly mown grass rolling into a thick belt of brush. A trampoline leaned near a battered soccer goal. Sensor lights ringed the house, with two floodlights on the corners, and a few outdoor cameras were mounted under the eaves.

Erin met them on the veranda with a smile that worked to stay steady. Dark hair tied back, average height, strong through the shoulders. Her grip was firm, but her eyes showed the strain.

"Thanks for coming," she said. "Kids are inside with Mum. My husband is on shift. I will tell you what I can."

"Appreciate it," Beretti said. "We know it is not easy."

They sat at the outside table. Erin kept both hands on a mug and watched the gully, tracing the rim with her thumb.

"It used to be fine out here," she said. "I grew up on this place. Nights were loud in a normal way. Frogs, the odd fox, a car on the back road. Then about a year ago it changed. Whatever is out there started showing up more, and you can tell when it is moving along the gully because every dog lights up, yard after yard like a siren. It usually comes from up toward Devil Monkey Mountain and runs down past us toward town. Cats went missing, a couple of little dogs too. Then the banging on the house started at two in the morning, hard enough to rattle a frame. You sit up and try to tell yourself it is wind, but you know it is not. Not when it starts to feel routine."

Ellis kept her tone even. "Any calls or sounds that are not knocks?"

Erin glanced at the fence line. "That is the bit I hate," she said, lowering her voice. "It called to my boys one arvo. Sounded like a cat in trouble, all friendly and whiny. They were near the fence, over there." She pointed. "I thought it was our tabby, so I did not jump straight away. They started toward the trees, I yelled, and the sound came again, deeper in. Not a cat. I knew it. I dragged them inside. Now they do not play out there unless me or my husband is right with them. Creepy as, honestly."

Jacobi nodded toward the cameras. "Those went up after the knocks started?"

"Yeah," Erin said. "They do not catch much. Shadows, little shifts. Sometimes in the morning one of them points the other way. We set them straight and by the next day one will be off again. We have checked the footage. You do not see a hand move it. It is like it knows."

"Have you had a clear look yourself?" Beretti asked.

"Only shapes," Erin said. "Tall in the trees, quick between the two gums down the back. My husband has seen more. One night it smacked the boards and he had had enough, grabbed the shotgun and went outside. He reckons it was standing behind his work ute at the tailgate, on two legs. Looked like a bloke and not a bloke. Dark hair all over, not glossy, just rough and flat. Eyes a red orange, too big for the face, and the mouth sat too wide. It let out a deep long growl that felt like a warning and then walked off along the fence like he did not matter. He is a steady sort, but he came inside and sat by the door till daybreak. The roofline on the Hilux is about six feet. He reckons it was two or three heads above that, so nine foot easy, maybe ten. Muscular but kind of stringy through here." She touched ribs and upper arms. "What rattled him most was how it moved when it left. He said it did not run tall. It hunched over, shoulders forward, arms swinging long, and it covered ground stupid fast. Made no sense for something that big. And the camera that would have had the angle had been twisted off the yard sometime that arvo, so of course we did not catch a thing."

Ellis drew a slow breath. "Has it stepped onto the veranda?"

"Twice," Erin said. "One winter morning we found wet prints. Bare like a person, wider and longer though, and there was a smear on that post. We saved a screen grab from another night, but it is murky."

"Anything recent?" Beretti asked. "Fresh enough that we should see it now."

Erin looked toward the yard and then back to the gully, a quick, nervous glance. "Yeah," she said. "Come on, I will show you."

They left the veranda and crossed the grass. The house sat high on stumps, so late light ran in bars beneath the floor. A steel rotary clothesline stood behind the house, the old Hills Hoist type that survives kids and summer storms. Erin lifted a hand toward it and kept scanning the trees.

As they rounded the corner, the smell hit first, hot and rancid in the heat. Flies swarmed in a dense cloud, and where tissue was worst a slow white wriggle had started along the torn edge.

An adult red kangaroo lay draped over one arm of the clothesline, placed with intent, its weight bowing the metal. The head was gone. The neck showed ripped muscle and stringy sinew where the vertebrae had been forced apart. The pouch was empty. One hind foot had snagged a line and pulled it tight, the wire giving a faint hum when the breeze shifted.

"Yesterday evening," Erin said. "About now, actually. I came out for towels and there it was. We have had dead, mutilated roos here before but not staged like this. I rang Hofner. He sent a car past after dark and told us to leave it until you came. I cannot stand it being there, but I did what he asked." She folded her arms, then set her hands in her pockets to keep them still.

Beretti pulled on nitriles and moved in a slow arc with her phone, catching the bend in the arm, the lay of the legs, the ragged neck stump. She stepped back for the wide frame, then checked the upright for smears. Dust and a faint greasy patch. Nothing clean to lift.

"Tracks," Jacobi said, already reading the ground. The grass around the pole showed wide scuffs with little depth, more from mass than stomp. He followed a path to a dusty patch that had held shapes in the shade. The spacing ran long for an ordinary stride. He crouched without touching. "Large and heavy," he said. "The dirt will not give us more than size and direction."

Ellis stayed with Erin. "Anything else out of place when

you found it?" she asked. "Tools, doors, gear."

"Peg basket tipped, clothes twisted, but wind does that," Erin said. "Cameras were suss again this morning. The back corner one had shifted."

"Do you think there is one or more?" Jacobi asked, still searching the near ground.

"We usually hear only one," Erin said. "Always one at a time. Could be the same visitor, could be different ones moving through. No one here knows."

"Is there anything out here that could take a head like that?" he said.

"Only a human with superhuman strength could," Erin answered. "But why would you, and why put it on my line? Either way it reads like a message to me."

Beretti peeled off her gloves. "Thanks for leaving it as is," she said. "We will coordinate with Haines about getting it down."

"Thanks, but my husband will do it," Erin said. "The boys will not look out the window while it is there."

"What made you mention it to your cousin who works in

the FBI?" Beretti asked.

Erin drew a breath, still watching the trees. "I was chatting online with my cousin one night. She is an FBI analyst. Alice. I told her I was creeped out and she asked why, and it all spilled out. I never thought she could do anything from the States. Then Senior Sergeant Haines rang and said two special agents were coming. I could not believe it. We feel helpless out here. No one has been able to help so far."

"We will do our best," Beretti said. "It is what we are trained for."

"Thank you," Erin said. She hesitated. "You two hunt these weird things, right?"

"You could say that," Jacobi said.

"So you are kind of like Mulder and Scully?"

He laughed. "Not really, but the comparison is nice. Great show. We tend to avoid the alien stuff and stick to cryptids."

Erin nodded once.

They walked back to the veranda. The smell thinned and the house gave them a little shelter from it. Erin poured water into glasses and set them out.

"Do you feel safe inside?" Ellis asked.

"Not like I used to," Erin said. "I would sit out here till late and never think about locking up. Now I do the rounds twice. I love this place. I have never wanted to live anywhere else. Lately I stand on the back steps and think about moving, and that breaks my heart. My GP has put me on anti anxiety meds for the first time in my life. I never thought I would need that, but here we are."

Beretti nodded. "Do you have any sense of why this has picked up? New work nearby, construction, logging, anything that might have pushed something out of a usual path?"

Erin thought it over and shook her head. "No. Not that I can think of. Nothing big has changed up our way."

"That is all right," Beretti said. "Sometimes we do not get a neat reason. A creature can start harassing or turn violent without a clean trigger."

"I hate that," Erin said. "But I get it."

"We are going to keep at it," Beretti said. "If anything happens, even if it feels small, ring us. Even if it is just a camera that turns."

"I will," Erin said. She met each of them in turn. "Do you

reckon those girls at the dam were taken, or was it a boating accident?"

Ellis did not tiptoe. "We are not sure yet," she said. "We are holding both possibilities open until the facts close one off."

Erin nodded and crossed her arms. "Please find out," she said. "Their mums are mates with my aunt. No one is sleeping."

Jacobi slid a card across the table. "If you or your husband remember something from months back that felt too small to bother the cops, ring anyway."

Erin tucked the card in her pocket. "Ta," she said. "And thanks for coming out. I know it sounds mad. Out here, it is just life right now."

They thanked her and stepped off the veranda. Late light trimmed the scrub and fell into the gully. A dog barked somewhere beyond the trees, another answered down the line, and the place settled again. As they crossed to the car, Beretti checked the nearest camera. The lens still faced the yard. She hoped it would stay that way until morning.

CHAPTER 13

Ellis eased to the curb outside the Airbnb and let the blinker tick. "Pub for dinner? They do a good schnitty and the beer's cold."

"What the heck is a schnitty?" Jacobi asked.

"Chicken schnitzel," she said, laughing. "Welcome to Australia."

"Tempting," Beretti said, unbuckling, "but I'm going to pile over my notes while they're fresh."

Ellis looked to Jacobi. "You?"

"I'm good. Rain check."

"Okay," she said. "You've got my number if you change

your mind."

Inside, they went straight to the table. Beretti opened her notebook and drew a clean two page spread.

"Let's lock the order," she said. "The dam happened first. After that we've got a run of things starting in the last two weeks."

Jacobi pulled in beside her. "Go."

"Maddie and Jamie," she said. "Phones gone and dead, tinny found drifting, no sign on shore. That's our oldest point."

"Last night lands between those," she said. "Well, technically this morning before 4am. Belinda and Jared on the edge of town. He sees a crouched figure at the window, freezes in the truck."

"Hunters hit between 4.30a.m. and 5.00a.m, dogs bolt, then it all goes bad. Cecil into a tree with a snapped neck. Stuey missing, likely killed. Three out and rattled."

"Erin's place caps the recent stuff," he said. "Calls to lure kids, knocks on the house, cameras turning, and a big red draped on the clothesline with the head ripped off and gone."

Beretti nodded. "Don't forget the shoe on Ellis's car. Clean and dry with the laces tucked inside."

Jacobi tapped his pen and sat back, thinking it through. "The yowie's playbook looks a lot like the sasquatch cases back home. Knocks on structures, mimic voice to draw kids, window watching, carcass display, hunched run with long reach. Same behaviors."

"Different ground, same behaviors," she said.

"Gotta make you wonder about origins, huh?" Jacobi asked. "Different countries and they get spotted all over the globe, just different versions of the same thing."

She clicked her pen. "That's a discussion for another time. Or perhaps the flight back home. Tomorrow afternoon, lets walk the gully behind the properties."

"Arvo," he said, grinning.

"Arvo, sorry," she answered. "And I think I will text Ellis and ask if the First Nations contact she has will drive out to Devil Monkey Mountain with us tomorrow. We'll need a decent four-wheel drive. Ellis's BMW is not going to handle off roading."

"Right. It's too precious for that," Jacobi chuckled.

Beretti sent the text. A minute later Ellis replied that she would call him and let them know. Ten minutes after that her name lit the screen. Beretti put it on speaker.

"Good to go," Ellis said. "He's in, and he has a four-wheel drive. We will be at your place at 2.pm."

"Perfect," Beretti said. "Thanks."

They hung up and Jacobi reached for his phone again when his stomach growled.

"Food," he said. "Not the pub."

He found a Chinese place in town that delivers with a quick search on his phone. "Mongolian beef, chicken and cashew, garlic greens, fried rice," he read. "You want anything else?"

"Salt and pepper squid," she said.

He ordered and set the phone down. "We've got a little time."

"Unknowns," she said, writing as she spoke. "Why the escalation. Erin doesn't see construction or logging pushing anything out, so that stays open. The sneaker. Message, trophy, or bait."

"Okay. Why the escalation?" he said. "Usual suspects:

people, land pressure, disease."

"Could be any of those, or something else," Beretti said.

She drew a thin line down the page. "In the morning, why don't we go for a drive and get the run of the land? Just ourselves."

"Sounds good. "I'll organize a rental car to be dropped off in the morning," Jacobi said, already pulling out his phone.

A knock at the door and "delivery" came through the flyscreen. Jacobi paid cash and brought the warm bags to the table. Garlic and chili lifted the room.

"Oh yeah," he said after a bite of squid. "Winner."

Beretti tried the chicken and cashew and nodded. "Exactly what I needed."

They ate from the containers, pushed them aside, and went back to the grid.

"That's it," Beretti said, closing her notebook. "I'm going to take a quick shower."

Jacobi finished the last of the fried rice and stood, stacking the containers. "I'll check the TV for anything interesting," he said.

CHAPTER 14

Jacobi woke to the hiss and thump of the coffee machine. He pulled on jeans and a tee and found Beretti at the kitchen table with her notebook open and steam rising from a mug.

"Wanna go for a walk and get some breakfast?" Jacobi asked.

"Hell yeah," Beretti replied.

"They dressed, freshened up, and were locking up within fifteen minutes."

As they walked along the footpath, the town was waking. A couple of utes idled outside the hardware store. Someone rolled a chalkboard out in front of a café. They took a table by the window.

"What's good?" Jacobi asked, scanning the board.

"Bacon and egg roll," the waitress said as she swung past. "Or avo on toast if you're feeling healthy. Flat white. Long black. Take your pick."

Jacobi leaned toward Beretti. "I'm assuming 'avo' is short for avocado?"

"Can't imagine what else," she said, amused.

"Flat white," Jacobi told the waitress when she came back, then pointed at Beretti. "She'll have a long black."

Beretti raised an eyebrow. "Are we ordering for each other now?"

"Only when I'm right," he said with a quick wink. "Two bacon and egg rolls as well. Add avo please." The waitress smiled, a faint flush touching her cheeks.

The food hit the table quick. They ate and watched the street draw a quiet map. School kids cut down the side lane with backpacks slung low. A council truck rattled over the bridge. Dogs worked their fences in short bursts and settled.

"Where first?" Jacobi asked, wiping his hands.

"I'm thinking the Vineyard," Beretti said. "The file flags a caretaker with a brief sighting last month. Let's talk to him first." She thumbed a text to Ellis for the address and to check his shift.

Her phone buzzed a few minutes later. "He is there," she read. "Ellis has let him know we are coming."

"Afterwards, we can check out the roads that shadow the gully," Beretti added.

"Sounds like a plan," Jacobi said.

They paid and headed back just as a late-model red Kia Stinger rolled to the curb. The driver stepped out with a clipboard. Beretti clocked Jacobi's grin.

"Are you serious?" she said.

"That was all they had left," he said.

"Right. Guess we won't be four-wheel driving in this."

"Mind if I drive first?" Jacobi asked.

"Go ahead," she said.

He jogged to the driver's door with a quick "thanks" to the rental guy and slid in. Beretti walked to the passenger side, smiling and shaking her head as she buckled in. The Stinger pulled away smooth and low, the cabin quiet enough that their voices felt close.

CHAPTER 15

Easing the Stinger out of town, Jacobi let it breathe through the gears while minding the limits. The road dropped into the vineyard valley, with straight rows and neat posts marching either side, netting in grey veils pulled back for the season. A couple of frost fans stood quiet on the ridge, blades stilled like windmills waiting for work.

Shane waited at the machinery shed, a lean bloke in a sun-faded cap and steel-caps, hi-vis shirt bleached almost white by years. He gave a quick nod, eyes already flicking to the back fence.

"Morning," Beretti said. "Special Agent Nicole Beretti, FBI. This is Special Agent Noah Jacobi."

"Shane O'Rourke," he said, shaking hands. "Officer Ellis

rang to say you'd be dropping by. I usually work nights, but I've been picking up a few hours in the day. Baby on the way, so every bit helps."

"Congrats," Jacobi said. "Rundown or walk first?"

"Walk," Beretti said. "Talk as we go."

They followed a service track between rows. Dripper lines ticked where a pump bled air. The ground had a skin of dust over hard clay. Magpies checked them from the posts and went back to prying at bugs.

"It was late," Shane said. "After lockup. Maybe ten. This was last month. I was doing a last pass because kids jump the fence for a laugh. I heard dogs along the gully start one by one, like a wave. Thought, here we go again. I'd been hearing that same chain for weeks but never saw anything. Killed the ute lights and took the torch. Saw something tall moving along the fence line. Not running fast. Just there, then over a row, then there again. Big. Could've been a tall bloke in gear, but it didn't move like one."

"Was there a smell?" Jacobi asked.

"Yeah," Shane said. "Like something left out in the sun. Roadkill, only different. I've never smelt it before. Hell, don't want to again. Couldn't get the smell outta my nose for hours."

They reached the back boundary where vineyard gave to a belt of tea-tree and paperbark. The fence wove along the gully edge, old wire stapled to hardwood posts, sections patched with newer mesh. A strip of bare earth ran inside the fence where tyres and boots had kept weeds down. The other side fell away into shadow.

Shane pointed with two fingers. "Here, right on the barb wire. Night after I saw it, we found a tuff of coarse, dark hair. It is long gone, now. Didn't think to keep it, sorry."

"Anything on cameras?" Jacobi asked.

"Nothing useful," Shane said. "Back corner cam didn't catch it. Wrong angle. Front cams picked up dogs going off and a bloke jogging at four, looks like the bakery run. That's it."

They eased along the fence to a pinch where a drainage cut met the mesh. Netting from the outer row lay torn and twisted into the wire, a strip hanging like a flag that never caught wind.

"That's new," Shane said. "We fixed the net last week. No storm since."

Beretti measured the tear against her forearm. "Height puts the rip above shoulder on an average man," she said.

"Edges are pulled, not cut."

"Any prints?" Beretti asked.

"Mostly smudged," Jacobi said. He crouched, careful not to touch. "Large impression. Edges smeared. Could be a double step. Direction pushes from the gully up into the rows, then back out again."

Shane chewed the inside of his cheek. "We've had strays hit the bins before. Pigs, roos, the odd feral dog. This is different. Dogs bark, then it goes dead quiet. Never used to feel like that."

"Tell us the rest of that night," Beretti said.

"On the way back to the shed I cut across the rows," Shane said. "Heard it come at me. Fast. Like it decided, right then. I didn't see it clean, just the rows shaking and that stink getting stronger. I threw the torch at the gap, ran for the ute, and backed it to the pad in record time. I got to the door of the shed and shoved it shut with my foot. Stood there shaking like an idiot for a minute. Scared the absolute shit out of me."

"Any livestock missing nearby?" Beretti said.

"Couple of goats up the hill last month," he said. "Old mate blamed dogs. I haven't seen dogs take heads."

They walked the line another hundred metres. A frost fan towered above the rows, ladder bolted, motor cowling locked. The posts here were newer. The mesh had a clean, wide bend, not a break.

"Pressure, not a cut," Jacobi said. "Something leaned or pushed to make space, then changed its mind."

Shane nodded. "Looks like it."

"Any staff spooked enough to quit?" Beretti asked.

"Yeah, now that you mention it." He scratched his beard. "The other caretaker who covered my shifts when I was off with the flu a few months back. Only six months in. He knocked off early one morning and never came back. Left personal gear in his locker; we had to post it. Wouldn't take the boss's calls. Felt off at the time, but I parked it."

"Sounds like he has a story he doesn't want to tell," Beretti said.

They turned back through the rows. A forklift sat penned near the shed. Bins were stacked in a neat wall throwing a hard-edged shade.

The wind shifted and brought that sun-soured reek up from the gully, faint but there. Dogs started up somewhere beyond the trees, two calls, then none.

"Well, thanks for your time, Shane," Beretti said. "If anything feels off, you call, even if it sounds silly."

"None of this sounds silly anymore," he said. "You take care looking for this thing. I wouldn't want your job."

They shook hands at the shed and headed for the car park..

They took the main road out and turned onto a quieter stretch behind a row of houses. Back fences gave way to a thick line of trees and brush, the gully sitting in a fold you could not see until the ground dipped. Every hundred yards another gate appeared, some locked, some not. The Stinger held the sweep cleanly, planted through the bends but firm over patched bitumen. On a clear straight, Jacobi leaned into the throttle just to feel it. The car stepped up in one clean move and settled again like it had been waiting to be asked.

The town thinned to small acreage blocks. Horses flicked tails at the edges of yards. A blue heeler trotted the fenceline, gave them one bark, and trotted back. A little farther on, the scrub pulled tight to the road and the gully came close enough that the air changed. Jacobi cracked his window and rested his elbow on the sill, letting the hum of the Stinger's tires fade under the sound of birds.

"Feels like a funnel here," he said. "If something moves this corridor, it will use the pinch. Less open ground, more cover, fewer eyes."

"I agree," Beretti said.

They looped along the back of the suburb where the gully pressed near sheds and boundary wire. A narrow service strip ran parallel to the trees, worn by foot traffic cutting the easy line. The Stinger's low nose made Jacobi ease the car over a shallow gutter.

The mountain sat farther off than it looked from town, not high as much as wide, with broken spurs shouldering into low country. Roads circled its base and cut away again in rough arcs. Jacobi kept them on clean bitumen. The Stinger liked it, settling into a steady hum and taking long curves like it wanted more.

They took a long sweep past the dam road and didn't turn in, only checked distance and the run of properties that backed onto that water. A few caravans sat on blocks behind chain mesh. A tinny rested half covered in a driveway with grass to the axles. A hand painted sign warned against trespass. The car stayed quiet at highway speed, tire noise lifting and dropping as the surface changed.

"Do you think that sneaker on the hood was placed there by the yowie?" Jacobi asked, breaking the silence.

"It makes sense," Beretti said. "If the yowie had something to do with their death."

On the way back toward town, they swung by the school and caught a narrow grass lane tucked between the oval and the start of the gully, just wide enough for a car.

"That's a night path if I ever saw one," Jacobi said. "The kind kids take to cut home and parents tell them not to."

Beretti nodded once. "Yep."

By late morning they had circled back toward the main street. They parked and walked past the shops. A couple of hunters from the pub stood by their ute and argued over something in the tray. One had bandaged knuckles and a bruised cheek. He saw them watching and looked away.

They grabbed an iced coffee and a banana muffin from a café and sat on a bench without saying much. At one, they headed back to the Airbnb to freshen up and pack for the afternoon.

CHAPTER 16

Beretti laid gear out on the table in tidy rows. Gloves, evidence bags, spare lights, notepads, camera, water, energy bars. She tapped the knife on her hip, a habit check, then clipped it back.

Jacobi checked his sidearm and holster. Beretti checked hers. They opened the weapons case and each ran a quick function check on their rifles, checking bolt, chamber, magazine, and safety, then zipped the case and set it by the door with the go bags.

"Ellis said two," he said, checking the time. "Got a few minutes to relax."

Beretti stood by the window and looked down the street, thinking through the next steps. "I think we should start at the mountain. It seems to be its home base," she said.

"Agreed," Jacobi replied as he sat on the couch with his phone and started scrolling through emails.

"You know," he said, "I've never met an Aboriginal person. I mean, an Australian Aboriginal."

Beretti looked over. "I think the term is First Nations people. But don't quote me on it."

He nodded. "Fair enough. I'm curious what his name will be."

She checked the window. "You're about to find out. They're here."

They grabbed their go-bags and rifle bags and stepped out. Ellis stood at the curb beside a white Toyota LandCruiser, talking with a shorter man who had a lean build, black hair threaded with grey, and a trimmed beard. Early forties, easy stance. He looked up as they approached.

Ellis made the introductions. "Special Agents Nicole Beretti and Noah Jacobi, this is Bob James."

Bob shook hands with both of them. His grip was firm without trying to prove anything. "Nice to meet you."

Jacobi's brow pinched a little. Bob caught it and smiled. "Let me guess, you were expecting a name you couldn't pronounce."

"Kind of," Jacobi said, thrown and honest.

"All good," Bob said, amused. "Mum is white. Dad's from my mob. I use my traditional name with family, but 'Bob' keeps things simple in town. Saves me spelling it out while someone has a panic."

"Appreciate you coming out," Beretti said.

"No worries," Bob said. "Ellis tells me you want a look around Devil Monkey way. I grew up knocking about those trails Although, it doesn't feel the same as it did back then I have to tell ya."

"I have heard that," Jacobi said.

Bob tipped his head toward the LandCruiser. "Pile in. She is old but keen. Nothing much stops a 'Cruiser out here. They live forever."

Ellis slid into the passenger seat. Beretti and Jacobi took the back. Bob started the engine, checked his mirrors, and pulled away.

"How long have you two been working together?" Bob asked as they rolled through town.

"About eight months," Jacobi said. "She leads. I keep up."

"That right," Bob said, grinning into the mirror. "Good on you, mate. Makes my job easier if you already know who listens to who."

Ellis looked back. "Plan is simple. We walk the mountain first, like you suggested Beretti. Bob knows the tracks and the fence lines. If we have time after that, we swing past the gully behind the properties."

"Copy," Beretti said.

Bob tapped the steering wheel as they idled at a stop sign. "Oh yeah. Watch your footing out here: holes, old fence wire, snakes. You definitely don't want to step on a king brown. You piss it off, its venom will kill ya before you make it to hospital."

Jacobi nodded. "Snakes. Great. Anything I should know beyond 'don't piss them off'?"

"That about covers it," Bob said, deadpan. "If you do, you'll know straight away."

Beretti hid a smile. "We appreciate the lift and the local knowledge."

"Happy to help," Bob said. "This is my backyard. If there is something roaming it and knocking people off, I want it sorted. Reckon you two brought the right toys for that."

"We brought enough," Beretti said.

"Good," Bob said. "Because if you run out of gear where we're going, the shops are a long walk."

They drove in a loose, comfortable quiet for a minute, the LandCruiser humming like it had done this run a thousand times. Bob glanced at Jacobi in the mirror again. "And mate, if it gets too bumpy back there on the dirt roads, sing out."

"Will do," Jacobi said.

Ellis checked her phone, then slid it away. "Haines wants a status update later."

"He'll be right," Bob said. "We will give him something worth the call." He flicked on the indicator and nodded ahead. "Track starts up there. After that, it is single lane and scrub. Hang on to your hats, boys and girls."

CHAPTER 17

The LandCruiser ate the last of the bitumen and shouldered onto red dirt. Brush closed in, fences fell away, and the track turned to a long rattle under the tires. A mob of wallabies broke from the verge and bounded through the scrub ahead of them, tails flicking as they vanished between the trunks.

"Small kangaroos?" Jacobi asked, watching them go.

"Wallabies," Bob said. "Same family, smaller build, different coat. You'll see both out here."

"Got it," Jacobi said.

"Devil Monkey Mountain," he added a moment later, reading a faded sign as it flashed by. "Think that name's about a yowie?"

"Could be," Bob said, easy at the wheel. "Never asked, to be honest. Names stick for all sorts of reasons."

He kept them going on the rough road. "Different mobs have different yarns. Some call it the hairy man. Sometimes it's a warning, sometimes it's a real fella in the scrub you don't go poking. Old people say you respect it. Don't chase it. Don't whistle at night. You listen to the dogs and your gut. Keep the kids close."

Ellis glanced across. "You seen it, Bob?"

"Seen enough tracks and shapes in the trees to put the hairs up on my neck," he said. "Nothing I'd write home about, ya know? But ya can't tell me we know of everything in the bush."

They bumped through a washout and climbed again. The scrub thickened, all vine tangles and pale trunks with scratch lines.

"I heard about Cecil's boys," Bob said after a minute. "Guess he didn't make it back."

"No," Beretti said. "Unfortunately."

Bob shook his head. "He was well known round here. In and out from way back. Reckoned he knew every gate worth jumping. Stir up the pub, take coin to push onto private land. That kind of bloke. To tell you the truth, I always thought he was a kangaroo short of the top paddock, but you didn't say that to his face."

Jacobi looked at Beretti, puzzled.

Bob saw it in the rear-view and grinned. "Means he had a screw loose, mate."

Jacobi smirked. "Got it. I like that one."

They rode another stretch in loose silence. The track pitched down through a dry creek and back up, then narrowed to two trenches with grass in the middle. After about two kilometres the LandCruiser ran out of room to be a car.

"All right," Bob said, easing to a stop. "Here we are. Wheels don't help past this. Everybody out that's good lookin'."

They stepped out into the hush that lives under big country. Bob lifted the tailgate. Beretti glanced at Ellis. "You had much experience with cryptids or anything like this?"

"Not a lot," Ellis said. "Had my fair share of strange,

though. More UFO calls and lights in the sky than I can count."

Beretti nodded and raised a rifle case to the edge of the tray. She and Jacobi checked chambers, optics, slings once again. Each checked their sidearm and slid it home. Backpacks up and snugged down. Ellis clipped her holster at her hip and ran a quick hand over spare mags and torch. Bob reached behind the seat for a weathered pump-action with scratches that had stories.

Bob looked them over and chuckled. "Reckon we're good for firepower, gang."

Jacobi caught Beretti's eye and grinned. Ellis shook her head, amused.

Bob swung the tailgate shut and pointed with his chin. "We'll skirt the ridge first, not straight up. Track's easier this way and you get more sightlines. We won't go all the way up the mountain, though. Too treacherous and hard walking for humans. If you hear dogs kick off down the gully, that's information. If the birds go quiet and the dogs don't, that's different information."

"You know the land," Beretti said. "We'll follow you."

"Too easy," Bob said. He locked the Cruiser, slid the keys

up under the rear wheel well, and told them where they'd be. He pulled a can of repellent from his bag, misted his arms and neck, then held it up. "Highly recommend you do the same." They sprayed down. Bob set a broad hat on his head, corks bobbing on twine to keep the flies off his face. Jacobi clocked it and thought, good idea.

Bob shouldered his pack and set off at a steady pace that kept breath easy and eyes up. They fell in one by one, boots biting into the slope, the bush folding around them and the track pulling them toward the spine of the mountain.

CHAPTER 18

They moved along the low side of the mountain in single file, the ground soft with leaf fall and the vine scrub catching their sleeves. Bob set an even pace and let the bush show the line. Flies found them, tested the air, and veered off once the repellent bit. The few that tried were chased off with a quick swish.

"Look up," Bob said, stopping at a young ironbark. "Nine feet, give or take."

A limb hung torn and twisted near the crown, fresh wood bright against old grey.

"Nothing big enough around here to do that," Jacobi said. "Well, other than one thing."

"Too clean for wind," Bob agreed.

They took photos and a quick measure off Jacobi's reach. Farther on, a smear of dark hair clung to a split cane where something broad had pushed through. Beretti eased the strands into paper envelopes, sealed them, and tucked them into her pack.

"Cruiser a good hour from here?" Jacobi asked as they walked.

"Bit less on the way back," Bob said. "We're angling, not climbing. And stick tight. There are old mines out here. Some holes you don't see until you're falling. People have vanished down them while hunting. If the scrub opens up in a weird circle, don't trust it."

"Noted," Beretti said. "We'll follow your footsteps."

They dropped into a shaded bend of a dry creek and the smell turned. Garbage and musk sat heavy under the vine mat. Bones lay in a scatter that made a rough fan against the bank. Roo mostly, some pig, a small jaw with a milk tooth still set. Long bones were split lengthwise with neat fractures. No skulls in sight. Above the pile, a strip of faded backpack webbing hung from a broken branch, half fused with spider silk.

"This place feels off," Ellis said, eyes moving. She rubbed her arms and stepped back like a shiver had walked through her.

Beretti crouched and went wide with the camera first, then closed in on the splits and the webbing.

Bob toed the edge of the pile without shifting anything. "Been here a while. Sun bleaching on the top pieces, dark underneath, webs layered across the better ones, leaf cast settled and stuck. Months at least, maybe more."

Jacobi lifted a rib with tweezers from his kit and checked the underside. "There's still a thin film of grease. That tracks with months."

Ellis eased the webbing free with forceps. "Looks like a pack strap."

"Bag it," Beretti said. "And take a couple of swabs off those splits, please."

They worked in silence. A goanna shuffled through the leaf litter not far off, froze with its head tilted, then slid like a shadow across the creek bed and disappeared.

"Heart stopped for a second," Jacobi said, letting out a breath. "Thought we had company."

"We do," Bob said, almost smiling. "That bloke minds his business."

They finished up and climbed out of the gully and took the bench again. The ridge bent them around a spur to a run of pale trunks where the ground turned from soft mulch to gritty sandstone. A narrow drag line crossed the surface and slipped into scrub, as if something heavy had been pulled single file. Bob crouched and pinched dust off the mark.

"Old," he said. "The ridge edges have softened and there's no fresh scuff over the top."

"What pulls that," Jacobi asked, "pig or person?"

"Could be either," Bob said. "No boot edges in the churn and no rope burn on the rock. Call it unknown for now."

They kept moving. At a fence remnant, three rusted posts held a slack run of barbed wire. A clump of dark hair sat on the top line at a height that made Jacobi step back and look again.

"That is high," Ellis said.

"Bag it," Beretti said. "Note the height while you are at it."

"How long have you been tracking, Bob?" Jacobi asked as

he worked.

"Since I could keep up," Bob said. "Uncles dragged me along before I could see over the bonnet. You learn to read country or you learn to limp."

Brush shifted to their right and they turned as one. A mob of kangaroos broke cover and ran, tails low and heads up, then bounded away through the trees.

"Just kangaroos," Bob said, lowering his hand. "We are fine."

A raucous cackle rolled from a nearby gum. Beretti and Jacobi both looked up.

"Is that a cookie... cooka... Pfft. I give up," Jacobi said, shaking his head.

"Kookaburra," Bob said, grinning. "Beautiful bird with a huge laugh."

"Fascinating," Beretti said.

They drank and pushed on, angling toward a wide shelf of rock. A few stubborn flies tested the repellent and they swatted and kept walking, conversation drifting in and out of the gaps.

"Those UFO calls you mentioned," Jacobi said to Ellis. "Any of them pan out?"

"Mostly lights with boring answers," she said. "A few did not, but not enough to hang your hat on. People see strange when they are already spooked. Sometimes the strange is real. Just follow the trail of multiple people have the same sighting."

"Same principle here," Beretti said. "Keep the possibles open and let the facts do the narrowing."

They stepped off the rock and into sandier soil. The smell shifted again, not the sour musk of the bone pocket but metal and dust. Bob slowed and pointed to a flat under a leaning bloodwood where the soil had darkened in a broad, uneven pool. Flies worked the edges without the frenzy of a fresh kill. The stain had dried to a deep brown-black with a thin crust. Scuff marks surrounded it as if feet or hooves had churned the ground. Two shallow grooves ran away into the brush like something had been dragged by the ankles.

"Not brand new," Ellis said. "But recent enough."

Jacobi held his hand near the edge. "Cracked skin on the surface and no tack. I would say days rather than hours."

Bob skimmed clean sand with a knuckle and showed a

faint red dust. "Wind has laid a film over the top and I do not see ants working the center. More than two days, less than two weeks. My money says wild pig. They smash each other up and you get pools like this when one loses in the wrong place."

"Could fit," Beretti said, studying the drag grooves. "Let's keep moving."

They angled away from the stain and took the high ground. The ridge rose and dropped in small folds that hid pockets where the air held still. At one fold Bob pointed to a shallow oval pressed into bark and grass under a low tangle, with entry and exit lines you could follow with your eyes.

"Fresh enough to hold shape," he said. "No leaf fall over the press and there is hair caught on the lip."

"Grab both points," Beretti said, passing him the envelopes. "Then we'll keep going."

They moved on, swapping small talk between checks.

"Back home," Jacobi said, "we get the rock throws and knocks. Different trees, same habits."

Bob nodded. "Different place, same playbook."

"Why put a bone pile where it did," Ellis asked. "Hiding or warning?"

"Convenience most likely," Bob said. "Dry, shaded, out of sight. Could serve both."

They walked until the light shifted toward evening and the ridge began to throw longer shade. A low rumble rolled in from a long way off, and another followed it a few breaths later.

"Was that thunder?" Jacobi asked.

Ellis looked up through the canopy. "Sounds like it. No storm in the forecast."

"Summer throws flash storms in a blink," Bob said.

"How far to the Cruiser?" Jacobi asked.

"We have come around the mountain," Bob replied with an edge or urgency. "About an hour if we continue this way. Let's get a move on."

CHAPTER 19

They filed down the slope, careful with each footfall as the ridge dropped into thicker scrub. Bob led, Beretti held the second slot, Ellis followed, and Jacobi brought up the rear. Clouds folded in and the light went flat and dark. The line kept tight, eyes on the ground and the edges.

A long, wild scream rolled across the slope. Not close, but close enough to land under the skin. It sounded like a woman in pain, though they knew it wasn't. It started high and fell off low at the end.

They stopped. Ellis turned in a tight circle, nerves up. "What was that?"

"That is what we are looking for," Beretti said, not taking her eyes off the trees. "Guns ready."

Metal and nylon whispered as they brought weapons up and reset grips. Ellis swallowed and reset her hold. "I felt that in my teeth," she said, eyes still searching the trees.

"Pick up the pace," Bob said. "Watch the ground."

They moved again, quicker but still careful where they put their feet.

"I don't think we're going to make it before it rains," Beretti said.

"Agreed," Bob answered. "We're going to wear it."

A few minutes later the sky opened. The rain came hard, hammering leaves and turning the clay to soap. A sharp, sour musk rode the rain for a breath and was gone.

"You get that?" Jacobi asked.

"Got it," Beretti said. "Eye's open, people."

They could not run. The slope was treacherous and the ground tried to slide out from under them. Twice Jacobi caught himself on a trunk. Ellis skidded, swore under her breath, and righted. Bob pointed them around a wet slab where moss waited to throw somebody. Mud latched on, then peeled off their boots with a wet tug, step after step.

They reached the lower trail and the footing steadied, but the canopy made it darker and dusk was closing anyway. Water ran along the track in braided streams. The rain fell in sheets that blurred everything beyond fifteen yards. Lightning flickered far off, then closer, and the world snapped white for a beat before dropping back into grey.

Jacobi brought his rifle forward. "This storm came on so damn quick."

"In summer, they do," Bob said, shotgun at a ready carry. "Good news is they're over pretty quick, usually."

"Usually," Jacobi mumbled.

Beretti shifted her rifle and took point behind Bob. The rain ate smaller sounds. It hid footsteps that were not theirs and made the bush feel crowded. Branches shook and flung water at them, each slap a false start. Thunder rolled after the flashes and made the ground feel close.

"Thirty minutes to the Cruiser if the track holds," Bob said.

They pushed on, heads down enough to see their footing, eyes up to read the edges. Lightning strobed again, throwing long shadows that jumped and vanished. In that pulse of light, Beretti saw the rain bend on a pale boulder upslope, the sheet breaking as if it struck something solid and then smoothing again. She fixed the spot and kept her eyes there as they moved.

A heartbeat later her shoulders went rigid. She lifted her chin into the rain, eyes locked right. "Your two o'clock," she said as she shook water from her face.

They slowed without stopping and slid a glance that way.

"On the large rock," she added.

Lightning hit and the ridge went white. On the boulder a mass the size of a bull lay on all fours, pressed flat as if doing push ups, elbows cocked high. The shape did not flinch at the light. It pressed flatter, like a swimmer taking a breath before a dive.

"What the hell is that?" Ellis said, wide-eyed, rain plastering her hair to her cheeks.

The flash died and the dark closed like a door.

Jacobi planted, shouldered, and fired into where the bulk had been.

Ellis turned, worry tight in her voice. "Did you hit it?"

"No idea," he said, scanning hard.

Lightning tore again and the rock was bare. Whatever had been there was gone.

"Watch your six," Beretti shouted over the rain. "It could be anywhere."

They tightened the file and moved, rifles forward with sidearm and shotgun guarding the rear. Bob kept his eyes working the edges. "That thing was enormous," he said, voice low. "Holy shit."

No one said a word.

The rain drove at them and the track narrowed between banks of scrub. Every splash, every branch snap, every clatter of a loosened stone sounded like a step that might mean something. They kept a steady pace toward the Cruiser, eyes sharp, mud tugging at their boots with every stride.

CHAPTER 20

Ten minutes from the Cruiser the track narrowed and tipped along a bank. Rain beat the scrub flat and came back in sheets. The line held tight. Bob first, Beretti second, Ellis behind her, Jacobi on the tail.

A rushing sound cut through the rain. Not wind. A hard whoosh that carried weight.

Ellis screamed and dropped, clutching her leg. A rock the size of a brick spun to a stop beside her, edges slick.

"Shit. You all right?" Beretti called, eyes on the trees where the throw might have come from.

Ellis tried to answer and only managed, "No."

"Bob, check her. Jacobi, take that side and watch for movement," Beretti said, shifting to cover.

Bob slid in, peeled Ellis's hands away from her calf, and swore under his breath. "It has taken a big chunk. I can see bone. Might be a fracture."

Ellis cried through clenched teeth. Rain washed pink down her boot and into the mud.

"We can't fix that here," Beretti said, glancing down and back up again. "Too wet and too exposed." She met Jacobi's eyes. "Can you carry her to the Cruiser?"

"Yes," he said, already slinging his rifle across his back.

"Bob, shotgun ready. You lead. Jacobi, lift her. We move on my word."

Jacobi bent to Ellis. "This is going to hurt," he said. "We are going to fix you up back at the truck."

He got an arm under her shoulders and another under her knees. When he lifted, Ellis screamed and sagged, breath gone. He shifted her to keep the ruined calf clear and found his balance.

"Go," Beretti said.

Bob took point, shotgun in a ready grip. Beretti moved on his hip, rifle up. Jacobi came in behind with Ellis, careful and strong, setting his feet through the mud's pull. Ellis hung on and fought to stay with them, breath hitching, face milk white.

Something hit the ground off their right shoulder with weight you could feel through your boots. Ten, maybe fifteen feet in, the scrub bowed and sprang back. Two heavy footfalls, then a breath of nothing that buzzed in their ears.

It came again from the left, closer. A quick two-beat rush that checked itself the moment the brush opened, like a charge pulled short. Leaves shivered. A twig snapped and the sound died as if swallowed.

"Oh, fuck me. I'm gonna shit my pants," Bob said, voice almost trembling.

"Just keep moving," Jacobi said through gritted teeth.

The footfalls hit again to their rear and fell silent. Rain hammered the leaves and made the bush feel tight to their faces.

After a minute Beretti said, "It is playing with us."

They climbed the lip of the track and pushed, each step a

tug and a wet release. Thunder rolled so close it seemed to come out of the ground. Lightning strobed and showed trunks, fern, a dark gap that might have been nothing or a shoulder turning away.

"Left bank," Bob said. "We keep the high side."

They took a tight corner where the track slid along a clay wall. Bob first, then Beretti. Jacobi stepped in, weight centered. Ellis braced, fingers locked in his jacket. The bank tried to throw him and he caught a root with his heel and rode it out.

"Okay, okay," Bob said without turning. "We can do this."

Lightning flared again and the trees opened to the small clearing they had walked out of that afternoon. The white LandCruiser sat fifty metres ahead, the shape of salvation.

"Move," Beretti said.

They went. A single stone hit the rear quarter panel with a deep note and dropped. The scrub on the far side shook once, like a heavy hand brushed through it, then fell still.

Bob dug the keys out as he ran, thumbed the fob, and the lights blinked. "Back left," he said. "Lay her across the seat."

Beretti pulled the rear door open, planted a shoulder to the Cruiser, and covered Jacobi while he eased Ellis onto the rear seat. Ellis gripped his sleeve and swallowed a cry.

"I have you," he said. "You are in."

"Jacobi front," Beretti said. "I am with her."

Bob scanned the tree line, slid his shotgun beside the seat, then climbed in and turned the key. The engine caught and settled.

Beretti ran around to the other side, ducked into the back beside Ellis, and tore open her pack. She blotted the leg with gauze, drying what she could without pushing into the wound. "You need a splint," she said, steady and calm. "For now this will stop the bleeding." She ripped a QuickClot packet, poured the granules straight onto the wound, and pressed them in with gauze until the flow slowed. Then she grabbed a plastic packet from her kit and looked Ellis in the eye. "Are you allergic to morphine?"

"No," Ellis said through her teeth.

"This will sting for a second," Beretti said. "It should take the edge off."

She pushed the dose. A warm wave moved through Ellis

and her body loosened, jaw unclenching, shoulders easing.

Bob sat wide-eyed as the Cruiser idled, ready to move, and Jacobi watched the mirrors and the treeline as thunder rolled over them again. When Beretti gave the go-ahead, Bob dropped it into gear and took off, leaving the clearing behind.

CHAPTER 21

Bob kept the wheel steady and worked the throttle like it was glass. The track had become ruts full of brown water and clay that wanted to keep them. Rain beat the windscreen so hard the wipers only carved brief windows that closed again.

"I have a funny feeling this road is going to be tougher to get through than any of us want to admit," he said.

The Cruiser slid sideways and came back. The rear fishtailed, caught, and fishtailed again. Tires spun and bit and spun again. Bob fed it just enough and eased it back into the ruts.

They rounded a bend into a straight stretch that looked better in the half light. The center held a long ribbon of slush.

Bob picked a line along the firmer edge. "Hold on," he said, and tried to carry speed past the worst of it.

The track turned to soup under them. The tyres spun. The Cruiser didn't budge. The nose sank a hair and stayed there. Bob lifted, set it back down, and tried again. The engine climbed and the wheels only polished clay.

"Not good," Jacobi said as he squinted through the windscreen.

Bob dropped into reverse and rocked it. Nothing. He feathered it, then gave more, then less, trying to feel for grip that was not there. The back end sank another inch and slurped.

"Try again," Beretti said, watching the windows and the tree line.

Bob took a breath and worked the shifter in a careful forward–reverse rhythm. He had little faith it would bite, but he tried anyway. The Cruiser shuddered, lifted a little, then settled like it had made up its mind. The smell of hot rubber crept in under the rain.

"It's no good," Bob said, frustration sharp in his voice, and he hit the wheel. "We're bogged."

"Shit," Jacobi said under his breath.

"Anyone got a signal?" Beretti asked.

They all checked. Three phones came up blank. Ellis did not need to look. She lay across the back seat with her eyes closed, breath slow and measured, the morphine taking the high edge off and leaving the ache.

"No bars," Jacobi said.

"Nothing here," Bob said.

They sat with the engine idling in the dark, stuck in mud with a creature out there that had already put a rock into one of them. Rain drummed on the roof. Water ran in sheets off the bonnet and down the side glass. The wipers kept up their metronome, two beats and a wipe, two beats and a wipe.

Beretti drew her sidearm and rested it low along her thigh. Jacobi did the same in the front passenger seat. He turned toward Bob. "You got a sidearm?"

"No."

Jacobi pulled Ellis's handgun from his belt, the one he had picked up after she was hit, and handed it across. Bob checked the action, checked the mag, and held.

His eyes stayed on the track ahead and the wall of black trunks beyond the beams. "What are we going to do?"

"There's not much choice," Jacobi said. "We sit tight. If someone comes through, great. Otherwise we wait for light."

Bob's jaw worked. "Light is twelve hours away! That thing is going to come for us." He blew out a tight breath. "I am going to piss my pants."

"Stay calm," Beretti said. "If it shows, we handle it."

Ellis swallowed and blinked, pulling herself up enough to listen. "I'm all right," she said, voice groggy. "If you're about to jump out and leg it, don't make me run."

"We are not running," Beretti said, gentle but firm. "We stay with the Cruiser."

"How much fuel?" she asked, eyes back on the treeline.

Bob glanced at the gauge and back up. "Three quarters."

"Good. Keep it running. Headlights stay on. Without them we would not see our own hands."

He nodded and left the beams on high. The light struck the rain and scattered, then reached the trunks and made them gleam. Steam curled up off the bonnet. The heater fought the fog on the windscreen and lost ground, then caught up again.

They locked the doors without ceremony. Inside it was controlled breathing, the tick of cooling metal, rain on the roof, the wipers' squeal, and water dripping from cuffs onto the mats.

Far out in the scrub a branch knocked against another and went quiet. Something shifted water in the ditch beside them and moved on. It could have been runoff. It could have been more. No one said so out loud.

Jacobi kept an eye on the mirrors and down the track as far as the beams reached. He kept the handgun low and loose in his hand. "If we lose the lights, we go to torches," he said.

"We won't lose them," Bob said, and then softer, as much to himself as to the others. "We won't."

Ellis breathed through a fresh wave and let it go. Sweat stood out on her forehead and ran into her hair. "Leg's hot," she said.

"That is the QuickClot," Beretti said. "Doing its job."

A minute stretched. Then another. The rain eased and came back heavier. The track glistened and the ruts filled to the lip. The brushes of the wipers ticked a little slower and then resumed their pace.

"Eyes open," Beretti said. "Nobody stares at one thing. Sweep and come back."

They watched the darkness beyond the beams and listened to the rain. The minutes drew long enough to feel. No one reached for a theory. They sat with what was true: a stuck Cruiser, deep mud, a wounded leg, and something in the trees that knew they were here.

CHAPTER 22

Two hours crawled by in the cab. The rain eased to a mist and then to nothing. Headlights threw two hard lanes down the track and died at the trees. Steam hugged the bonnet. Inside the Cruiser the heat built and faded in slow waves as the fan clicked between settings. No frogs. No cicadas. No night birds. The bush wasn't giving away its secrets.

They kept the cabin dim. Flashlights came up one at a time in quick sweeps, then went dark again to save batteries. Every crack of a branch put nerves on edge and left them there.

"Think it's worth me getting out to find a log," Jacobi asked quietly, eyes on the ruts, "something to wedge under the tires?"

"No," Beretti said. "Too risky. You'll just give it a target."

Bob hunched over the wheel even though they were not moving, as if posture alone could tow the Cruiser a few inches toward town. Jacobi watched the mirrors and the place where the beams died. Beretti sat twisted toward the rear, one knee on the seat, one boot on the floor, sidearm low and ready. Ellis lay back with her eyes closed, breath even, a hand resting over the bandage.

"Just so you know," Bob said, eyes forward, "I did *not* piss or shit my pants. Nearly, but I held it."

Jacobi's mouth tugged into a small smirk. "Good to hear. We would know."

Ellis let out a thin breath possibly a laugh. Bob gave a quick nod and went back to watching the track ahead.

The strike on the side window came without warning. A crack like a bat on a bottle, a slap of cold air, and the sting of glass on skin. The pane beside Ellis blew in and a rock thudded off Beretti's thigh before dropping to the floor mat.

"Ellis screamed and folded; shards rattled across the rear seat and into the footwell, settling in the upholstery creases and the door pocket."

"What was that? What the hell was that?" Bob barked, jerking around in his seat.

"Rock," Jacobi said. "Don't lose it Bob. We are safer in here than out there."

"Safer? We are sitting ducks."

"Stay calm," Beretti said, voice steady. "It wants you to get out and run."

Cold, wet air poured through the broken frame and pushed the smell of bark and clay into the cab. Beretti leaned in to Ellis. "You okay?"

Ellis nodded, eyes squeezed shut.

"Lucky you had your face down," Beretti said. Keeping one eye on the brush through the broken window, she worked gently through Ellis's hair, picking out bright shards and brushing the grit from her scalp and collar.

Jacobi lifted his light and swept the scrub where the throw should have come from. Drops flared like sparks. Nothing moved. He killed the beam before it wrecked their night vision.

"You good?" he asked, looking back at Beretti's leg.

"'I'll be fine," she said, jaw tight. "Thanks for asking."

Ellis kept her head turned away from the opening, tears running. "It can just reach in and grab me."

"If anything comes that side," Beretti said, "stay down. I will be shooting."

"Copy," Ellis whispered, pulling her left knee in closer and keeping her head low.

They waited. The bush went flat again. Water tapped a slow rhythm down the inside of the broken frame.

Then weight hit the scrub to their right with speed and anger. Brush thrashed, trunks thudded in quick succession, and the ground fed a low shake through the seat rails.

Jacobi had the flashlight up before the small limbs stopped moving. Beretti lifted hers at the same time. Their beams cut the verge and met in wet leaves at shoulder height.

The rush stopped at the wall of light. It checked itself just outside the hard edge. Branches shivered and flung water. The trunks eased back. Nothing stepped into the beams. It had come in fast and quit fast, as if the light were a fence it chose not to cross.

They held the beams steady, breath marking time. The silence after had a thin metal tone in it, almost too faint to hear and too sharp to ignore.

Jacobi lowered his light a fraction. "It knows where the beams stop."

On a barely audible count of three they dropped the lights together. The tunnel of the headlights owned the track again.

The next rush came from the left, same weight, same speed, same last-second stop just outside what they could see. Leaves shook and dumped their load. Something big exhaled in a long push. No shape showed.

"There are two," Bob said, voice high.

"Just the same one," Beretti said. "Crossing behind us, staying out of the light."

Ellis whispered a prayer under her breath and held her hands together so tight her knuckles went white.

A deep growl bled out of the bushes on Ellis's side. It crawled along the skin and sat in the chest, low and ugly. It held steady for a count and faded like a bad engine winding down.

Beretti snapped her flashlight onto the sound and drove the beam into the scrub. The leaves flared and went flat again. No shape. From deeper in the trees came the heavy drum of something running away, long strides that ate ground and then vanished.

Silence folded over them again.

"How do you do this for a job?" Bob asked, shaking his head, voice unsteady. "This is insane."

"Just breathe through it," Jacobi said, keeping his pistol angled low and his flashlight near the sill. "If it comes in, we light it and we work it. Until then, we hold."

Bob stared into the tunnel of headlights.

Minutes stretched without a mark to show for them. Water ticked from the headliner over the broken frame and ran a line down in the door. Beretti pulled a spare shirt from her pack and tucked it into the jagged edge to slow the drip and deaden the glass.

"Thanks," Ellis whispered.

"You got it," Beretti said.

They settled into a rhythm. Quick sweeps with the lights. Mirrors. Tree line. No chatter. The bush answered with small marks: a twig snap on the right, a wet squelch on the left like a foot pulling free, a breath that did not belong to wind. Each time it stayed just beyond what the beams could give.

The rush came straight up the track then, inside the tunnel. They felt air shove at the front of the Cruiser. Leaves whipped and curled. For one breath the wet trunks had a taller shape layered over them, wrong and there. It slid out of the light faster than the eye could hold and veered left at the edge. The night soaked up the noise and kept it.

"It knows the edge," Jacobi said. "Every damn time."

Ellis let out a soft sound like half of a sob. "Please go away," she said to no one in the car. "Please."

The creature did not go. It stayed just outside their reach and tested the circle again and again. The smell swung in on a small change in wind, rank and thick, then thinned. Jacobi and Beretti lifted their lights together, held them at the edge, and waited. The smell grew, held, and did not cross. Ten feet. Always ten feet.

"Still one," Beretti said, quieter now. "Still testing."

They dropped the beams and went back to the tunnel.

The clock on the dash clicked one more minute forward. Somewhere behind the trees a single frog tried one note and thought better of it.

They watched the dark and listened to the rain coming back in a soft patter. The minutes stretched.

Bob cleared his throat. "How did you two end up hunting monsters?"

"Speaking for myself," Jacobi said, "you kind of fall into it. They pick you. If you can keep your cool after seeing one of those things, you get to stay." He glanced at Beretti. "Do you agree?"

"Pretty much," she said. "I also grew up with them on the family property."

"Yikes," Bob said. "Hard to picture seeing one as a kid. Kind of ironic you ended up hunting them."

"It is ingrained in me now," Beretti said.

"I have to hand it to you both," Bob said. "You've got balls of steel."

Jacobi snorted. "The trick is pretending we know what we're doing."

Beretti smiled. "Jacobi's right. Plus, having a stunning lack of self-preservation helps too."

The laughing loosened the air for a minute. Then the quiet settled back in and they remembered where they were and what was toying with them.

CHAPTER 23

The night dragged. Hours stacked without shape. Wind moved through the trees and then faded. Headlights threw two hard lanes down the track and died at the timber line. Inside the Cruiser the heat built and fell. No frogs. No cicadas. No night birds.

Ellis drifted, woke on a spike of pain, and drifted again. When her breath went sharp, Beretti drew another dose from the kit and pushed it slow. Ellis settled, eyes unfocused, jaw unclenched. Beretti adjusted the pack under her calf and watched her face until her breathing evened out.

They were tired, but Beretti and Jacobi held the line. They traded quick sweeps with the flashlights, kept voices low, checked fuel and battery.

From the dark, Bob said, "I have been trying to figure out what it smells like. All I picture is twenty dirty nappies left in the sun, rotten meat, a wet dog that has not seen a bath in years, and a splash of vinegar."

"That is oddly specific," Jacobi said, "but pretty on point."

Jacobi glanced at the gauge. "How long until the gas runs out?"

"Fuel," Bob said, eyes on the dark. "Big tank. At idle, about twenty-four hours. That is not a worry, mate."

"My missus knows we are out here," Bob added after a moment, eyes closed, head on the headrest. "No way she would try to come in. She would know this road is mush." A beat. "Best we can do is walk at daylight. This track will not dry until the sun is on it for hours."

Beretti shifted and her thigh lit where the rock had landed, a hot coin under the skin. She breathed through it and kept scanning. Jacobi rolled his shoulders once and reset his grip, counting breaths to keep the tired out of his hands. Bob kept his boot flat on the floor, toes inches from the brake, ready.

The footfalls came up behind them like a drumline built from bone. Heavy. Even. Bipedal. Each step landed with a wet, sucking slap, mud squelching and water sloshing in the ruts. The first hit tingled the floor under Bob's boot; the next walked up the chassis, a slow drum that settled in their ribs. A push of air came with it, and a long, steady breathing that belonged to something with a barrel chest.

Something tapped the tow hitch. Not a knock. A slow, testing press that made the rear springs groan.

Beretti did not turn. "On my count of three," she said to Bob, voice low. "Put your foot on the brake."

"Okay," he said.

"Everyone cover your ears."

Jacobi slid his hands up. Bob raised his boot over the pedal. Ellis pressed her palms to her ears and bit down on her lip. The thing shifted behind the Cruiser. A low growl pooled close to the tailgate and held there.

"Three," Beretti said, just above a whisper.

Bob pressed the pedal. Red filled the rear glass and splashed across the track. Beretti turned in her seat. In that wash she caught the breadth of a torso at window height, wet hair clumped with clay and burrs. A forearm the size of a fence post braced on the tailgate, a hand spread wide, nails sharp and split, clay packed in the creases. The panel flexed a fraction and came away with a smear the color of the track.

She fired three times through the back window. The glass burst outward. The cab went white-red with muzzle flash. Hot brass pinged off the middle console and one case kissed Beretti's forearm before it fell to the mat. Powder smoke folded into the warm air and stung the backs of their throats.

The shape jolted at the first round. The second shot pulled a sound like breath punched out of a chest. Then it launched for the trees before the glass shards finished falling. It screamed as it ran, a high, tearing sound that fell off into something deeper and vanished.

For a few seconds all they had was the ring in their ears and the patter of glass settling into the door seams. The red glare thinned, and the dark felt closer than before.

Jacobi kept his pistol low and scanned the tunnel of red. "Sounds like you hit it."

"I think so," Beretti said, breath steadying. "Hopefully enough to make it think twice about coming back for another try."

Bob sat turned in his seat, staring through the broken rectangle where the glass had been. "My missus is gonna kill me. This is her car," he said, louder than he meant to, ears still ringing from the gunfire.

"Don't worry, buddy," Jacobi said, still watching the dark. "It will get taken care of. What counts is we make it out of here alive."

Ellis swallowed, blinked, and let the morphine pull the edges off the spike in her calf. "I want to get out of here."

CHAPTER 24

Bob jerked awake with a snort and blinked at the windscreen. Grey light had rinsed the track. He glanced at Jacobi, still scanning the bush outside, then back to Beretti, doing the same.

"Guess I dozed off," he said, rubbing his face. He checked the dash. "Five forty-six."

"It has been quiet," Jacobi said. "Except for the snoring."

Bob scratched his jaw, a little embarrassed. 'Ah, yeah. Sorry about that. The missus says it's like a freight train bearing down.

Ellis slept in the back seat, cheek turned toward the door, breath soft and even.

While Bob was out, Beretti and Jacobi settled on a plan.

"Bob, we've got a plan," Jacobi said, voice even. "You and I walk until we hit a signal. Beretti stays with Ellis. We call it in and come straight back."

Bob nodded, then frowned. "Leaving you two here sits wrong."

Jacobi gave a short laugh. "She can handle her own and then some, buddy."

He hesitated, then nodded. "All right."

They ran it once more. Jacobi would carry his rifle and sidearm; Bob his shotgun, with Ellis's handgun tucked at his belt. They would follow the track back to the main road, skirting the worst of the slop and taking the high side where it held. Once they hit bitumen, the phones should have signal. They would call it in, get a lift back with whoever reached them first, and return straight to the Cruiser.

Jacobi popped his door. Cold air rolled in. He stepped out, slung the rifle, checked his holster. Bob climbed out on his side, racked his shotgun off-safe, settled Ellis's pistol in the waistband under his jacket.

Jacobi leaned back in. "We will be back as soon as we can."

"Keep your eyes open," Beretti said.

Before he stepped away, Bob reached in and clicked the headlights off. The cab fell into the soft grey of morning.

They started down the track with their weapons ready, boots finding the high spots, shoulders angled into a light wind.

The quiet settled as soon as they were gone. Beretti checked Ellis, then swept the tree line. The fuel needle had barely moved. Minutes slid past and stacked into an hour. A little more. Ellis woke once and drifted again. The first birds finally tried a few notes.

An hour later an engine note rolled in from far off. Not a sedan. Something with grunt. Beretti sat up and watched the mouth of the track. The sound grew, cut once, returned, and then a jacked-up Toyota Hilux eased into view, backing toward them. It came slow, chewing the mud with wide, blocky tires and walking the ruts like steps.

It pulled up nose-out in front of the LandCruiser, tyres tall and knobbly. A mate of Bob's sat at the wheel, blond hair tucked behind his ears, a grin under it. Bob rode shotgun; Jacobi leaned forward from the back and gave a quick wave.

Beretti stepped out to meet them. "Glad you found a

monster truck," she said, eyeing the height and those tyres.

The driver hopped down, lanky and loose. "How ya goin'? I'm Josh. Heard you had a night of it."

She shook his hand. "Appreciate the help."

"No dramas," he said. "We'll have you out in a tick."

He worked fast. Heavy strap to the Cruiser's front hook, a second line for angle, a quick look under the nose. Bob slid behind the wheel of the LandCruiser. On Josh's nod, Bob gave it a touch while the Hilux eased forward. The strap tightened, sang, and the Cruiser climbed out of the suction with a wet pop and a shudder. Josh pulled a few metres more until the ground firmed.

"Too easy," Josh said. "Let's get you to the blacktop."

Before they moved, Beretti climbed into the rear of the Cruiser beside Ellis, hands on her leg to keep it steady. They rolled out in a slow convoy: the Hilux towing with a steady pull, Bob keeping the Cruiser straight, Jacobi in the back of the ute calling the line when needed. Every bump drew a grunt from Ellis. The main road opened under a pale sky, and an ambulance waited on the shoulder with beacons on low flash.

Paramedics jogged over as they stopped. They moved

quick, checked Ellis's leg, asked her name, got the basics, slid her onto a stretcher. She answered, voice raspy with pain, and gripped the rail.

One of the ambos looked up at Beretti. "You want a quick look? You're limping."

"I'm okay," she said. "Hot shower and sleep will do me fine."

"All righty then," he said, turning back to tape a line.

Jacobi stood off to the side, watching without getting in the way. He caught Beretti's eye. "House. Shower. Then Ward."

"Agreed," she said.

They thanked Bob and they thanked Josh again. Jacobi slid a card from his wallet and handed it to Bob. "Windows on the Cruiser," he said. "Reach out. We'll sort it."

Bob tucked the card into his shirt pocket. "Appreciate it."

"Jump in," Josh said, thumbing toward town. "I'll run you back."

They climbed into the Hilux. Bob eased the LandCruiser toward home. The ambulance rolled for Fairwater, a twenty-minute drive away. Josh pointed the lifted rig at town, the big tires humming on the gravel, and carried them toward hot water, a bed, and the call to ASIC Ward that would take some telling.

CHAPTER 25

Nicole walked out into the living room and sat on the couch. Sun pushed at the blinds. The clock on the stove read one in the afternoon. Her thigh reminded her of the rock with a tight, mean ache. She sat and let the house come back into focus. Quiet street outside. A bird somewhere hitting the same three notes.

Twenty minutes later Jacobi padded in, hair a little wild, T-shirt twisted at the collar. He dropped into the chair across from her and gave her a look that took stock without being a fuss.

"How's the leg?"

"Pretty sore," she said. "I will live."

He nodded. "Any sleep?"

"Enough to stand up straight," she said. "I have an idea."

"All ears."

"We go back to the gully," she said. "Set up on the opposite side from where we were yesterday. You pitch a small tent like you are just another camper. Lantern, a chair, a cooler. I take the high ground above you on that slope and wait it out. If it gets curious and comes in, I take the shot."

He rolled it around, then lifted his eyebrows. "So I am the bait?"

"Yes."

He grinned. "Best idea I have heard all trip. No wonder you are the boss."

She chuckled and pushed herself up. "I am not your boss, Jacobi."

"Hell, yeah you are," he said. "Would not have it any other way."

"When do we do it?" he asked.

"As soon as possible," she said. "Coffee, then gear."

"On it."

Jacobi went to the counter and woke the machine. He bled the line, locked in a basket, and pulled two long blacks. Beretti tested her leg, stretched without pulling the bandage, and went to the bedroom to dress. She chose clothes that would disappear against scrub and shadow, then checked her pack: fresh batteries, optics, spare tourniquet, extra gauze, two full mags, and a radio and ear piece. From their agency case she added two sets of night-vision goggles and spare mounts.

"You want sugar?" he called over the hiss.

"No, thanks."

A knock sounded at the door.

Beretti opened it. "Senior Sergeant."

"Haines," he said with a small nod. "I will not keep you long."

Jacobi met them in the living room and set the coffees on the table.

"We found Stuey this morning," Haines said. "Stuffed into a rotted log and fed upon. Horrible sight."

"That is horrible," Beretti said.

"Uggh. At least they found him, for his family," Jacobi added.

"Sorry I have not been around more," Haines went on. "You were in good hands with Officer Ellis. Unfortunate what happened to her last night. I spoke to her on the way here. She is sore but better."

"We understand and we are glad she is feeling better. She is a strong officer," Beretti said.

"Yes, she is. As you can probably guess, my team is stretched thin," Haines said. "We cover more than eighty kilometres with not enough boots. People here have asked for a station for years. Powers that be say there is no budget."

Jacobi nodded. Beretti outlined their plan for the afternoon. "We will set a tent at the campground, low profile. I will take high ground across the gully and watch. If it approaches, I will engage."

"All right. Keep me looped," Haines said.

"Before you head off," Beretti asked, "have you ever seen a yowie?"

He paused, weighing how much to give. "I guess I can say it to you two. Sixteen years ago. Small town called Killcoy, about forty minutes from here. One stood on the side of a back road as I drove past. Tall. Still. Watching me. I was a young constable. I kept it to myself."

"How did you know to ask?" he added.

"You get a feel for people in this job," Beretti said. "Not many senior sergeants are comfortable with the FBI walking into their town. You were. That usually means they have seen more than the average."

"I welcome the help," Haines said. "If it saves another life, I am all for it." He moved to the door. "Good luck this arvo."

"Thanks for coming by," Beretti said.

He tipped two fingers and stepped out.

She came back and took the mug from Jacobi, warm in both hands. He had a map open on his phone, not for directions, just to think. He pointed with his chin. "That bend opposite yesterday's route. There is a shelf with a view. You set up above it. I pitch a tent down in that small clearing. If it comes along the gully, it sees the tent first."

"That works," she said.

"Copy. "We do need to buy a tent, though. And a cheap

chair and a battery-operated lantern. Store in town?"

"Outdoor shop on Main, I think," she said. "We'll swing by."

"And the pie shop?" he asked, hopeful.

"Good idea. Fuel for the stakeout."

****

Haines had just pulled the patrol car door shut when the radio cracked to life. Windows up. Air con on.

"Control to Senior Sergeant Haines. A local male has presented at station with a sighting this morning. Says it is unusual. Requesting you."

"Copy," Haines said. "Twenty-five minutes."

He turned the wheel and headed back through town toward the Fairwater.

****

Jacobi finished his coffee and set the mug in the sink. "Tent, chair, lantern, cooler. I will load the Stinger."

"Can you grab the second radio," she said. "Please."

He saluted with two fingers and headed for the door. She zipped the pack, checked the NVGs once more, and listened to the trunk thump open.

"Ready?" he called.

"Ready," she said, shouldering the pack.

They met at the door and took one last look around the room out of habit. Beretti turned the lock and pocketed the key.

CHAPTER 26

A man sat in the waiting chairs at the police station, about fifty, curly black hair, weathered skin, slim build in a T-shirt and shorts. He stood as Haines walked in.

"Hi, Senior Sergeant. Tony Marino," he said, holding out a hand.

"Tony," Haines nodded and shook his hand. "This way."

In Interview Two, Haines set a small recorder on the table. "This is Senior Sergeant Luke Haines. I am recording. Do you consent to this interview?"

"Yeah," Tony said. "All good."

"Please state your name."

"Tony Marino."

"What brought you in?"

"Most weekends I pick for the markets," Tony said. "Tomatoes, zucchini, eggplant, capsicum. Same as always. Loaded the little Isuzu. My daughter, Zina, came with me. She is sixteen. We were on Old Dandenoo Road, just past the old dairy. Sun was just up. Bit of mist sitting low in the paddocks, nothing unusual, right?"

His fingers played with the hem of his shirt. He took a breath that did not quite make it.

"Take your time," Haines said.

"Windows were down, radio on," Tony went on. "Nice breeze. Then this stink hits us. Proper rancid. You expect a smell off the paddocks, right? But this was worse than anything I have ever smelled. I was about to say, 'What is that?' when I see something in the corner of my eye. Out in the field. On two legs. Heading for the road. I think, all right, some poor bugger sleeping rough. Then I see it is covered head to toe in hair. Dark, filthy, matted, stringy."

He swallowed, looked at the table, and blinked fast.

"I slow the truck," he said. "It is not even looking at us. I would have hit it otherwise. What put the wind up me was how it was acting. Scratching at its chest, trying to reach its back like it had ants under the skin. And it was talking. Not to us. To itself. Fast. Not words I know. Just this run of sound. Would not shut up, and it sounded angry."

"You thought it might be a person," Haines said.

"For a second," Tony nodded. "A really tall feral off his head. That is where my head went. But it just walked across the road in front of us. Another car came the other way. They slowed too. We both watched it cross and slip into the scrub like it knew the gap. I looked at the other driver. They had the same look I did. Then they took off. Foot down."

He pressed thumb and forefinger into the bridge of his nose.

"My girl started crying," he said quietly. "Not loud. Just upset. Said she felt crook. I felt it too. Not the stink. The feeling. Like we had seen something we were not supposed to."

"What else did you notice?" Haines asked. "Height. Smell. Any sound besides the talking."

"Smell was bin-in-the-sun with wet dog and something sour," Tony said. "It was taller than me by heaps. I am five ten. I had to lean closer to the windscreen to see its head as it went past, and it crossed maybe twenty metres in front of us. Broad across here." He set his hands at ribs and shoulders. "The talking did not stop even while it crossed. Like it could not shut up. You could hear it, clear as day."

He looked up, meeting Haines's eyes. "This the thing people are on about? The yowie."

"Sounds like it," Haines said.

"We never made the markets," Tony said. "My daughter was too shaken. Me too, if I am honest. We went to my brother's on the other side of town. He said come in and tell you. I do not care if people talk. I just want it on the record that it is still out there. Even though it acted like we weren't there, it did not feel friendly."

"Thank you for coming in," Haines said. He clicked the recorder off. "I appreciate it."

They stood. Haines shook his hand. "Take it easy today. We will run cars through that area."

Tony shook the senior sergeant's hand and left the room.

In the quiet office, Haines thumbed his phone and typed a message to Beretti:

Sighting this morning. Old Dandenoo Rd just after first light. Male with teen daughter. Tall, fully haired biped crossed about 20 m ahead, paddock to scrub. Strong odour. Vocalising to itself, sounded angry. No approach, no injuries. Will update after your stakeout. Not urgent.

He sent it, slipped the recorder into the evidence tray, and headed back out to the car. The station doors shut behind him with a soft click that felt louder than it should.

CHAPTER 27

As Jacobi climbed back into the Stinger outside the camping store, Beretti read Haines's text aloud: sighting just after first light on Old Dandenoo Road, tall fully haired biped crossing from paddock to scrub, strong odour, mumbling to itself and sounding angry, no injuries, not urgent.

Jacobi nodded, already into the first of two pies. Beretti had eaten hers fast so the smell would not cling.

Jacobi eased the Stinger onto the verge and Beretti stepped out with her pack and rifle. She pointed him on and took the goat track that cut up through the scrub.

As she rounded the first bend, she dabbed earth-scent along her wrists and collar, smeared a thin rake of mud over exposed fabric, tucked her hair into a cap over a tight bun, and checked the wind again.

He rolled on to the small campground pull-in a few hundred yards along the gully. He parked by two empty picnic tables and a rusted drum barbecue, moving the way any lone camper would. From the boot he pulled the new two-man tent, a cheap folding chair, a lantern to hang as a prop, and an empty cooler.

Over the comm in his ear, Beretti came through clear.

"I have you," she said. "Right of you, high ledge behind the scrub. I can see the whole flat."

"Copy," he said. "If anything walks in, you will catch it first."

She lay prone on a rock shelf under thick brush, rifle on its bipod, stock tucked, cheek weld set, glass sweeping the campground in slow arcs. It would be a long wait. That was fine. Patience was part of her kit.

Jacobi pitched the tent like he had done it a hundred times, shoulders loose, no hurry. He staked the corners, ran the poles, left a flap half open.

Something soft tapped the rock near her elbow. Another

piece dropped, then another. Beretti looked up. A koala was wedged in a fork of the nearest gum, chewing through fresh leaves and staring down at her. "Well if that ain't damn cute," she mumbled, then slid her eye back to the scope.

He set the chair and cooler where they would be seen from the track and hung the lantern from the tent door, dark. From a paper bag he pulled the pies they had saved and took a bite that made him close his eyes for a beat.

"You kept the steak and pepper," Beretti said, amused.

"I kept two," he said. "One for now, one for later."

"Greedy," she said, and he could hear the smile.

He finished dressing the scene and settled into the chair with a paperback for cover. The book stayed closed on his knee. They let the small talk run in quiet threads and then gave it space. A magpie carol drifted and faded. The light shifted a shade.

"Wind still good," she said. "Down gully."

"Copy."

Time stretched. Jacobi took careful sips from a water bottle and let the chair creak like an ordinary camper shifting for comfort.

They were mid-conversation about nothing at all when Beretti stopped speaking. Static filled the space her voice had been.

"Talk to me," he said, keeping his head still.

"Snake," she said.

Everything in him went quiet. "Color?"

"I do not know. I am not moving. I do not want a bite."

"Stay still," he said, voice low and even. "Breathe shallow. Let me know when it goes."

Heat pressed under her clothes. The ground touched her everywhere at once. She could hear it before she felt it, a dry whisper of leaf litter parting, then the slow, certain slide of weight that was more muscle than noise. The first contact came at her boot, a cool line finding the lace and pausing there. The tongue flicked once, a soft tap against leather, and withdrew.

She kept her chest locked and let the rifle bear the weight of her arms. The thing eased along the outside of her ankle, ribs counting themselves against her, each plate a tiny pressure. It followed the seam of her pants and laid its body across both lower legs as if they were a warm log. She set her eyes on a fixed point in the leaves and did not blink. Sweat pooled at her temple, crawled along her cheek, and into the mud at her jaw.

It stayed there long enough for her pulse to climb into her throat. Somewhere below the ledge a fly buzzed and went still. The snake's body shifted, a patient inch at a time, scales rasping with a sound like paper rubbed between fingers. Its tail slid over one boot, then the other, and lifted free.

She let herself take a breath. Only her eyes moved. Off to the right, a long brown body eased into the leaf litter and threaded between roots, head low, tongue tasting the air.

"Holy shit," she whispered. "Clear."

"Copy," he said. "Good job."

The quiet returned as if it had been waiting a few feet away. He let a slow minute pass before he spoke again.

"With our luck," he said, "we won't see any Yowie action until dark."

"Probably," she said.

"How tall do you put this one?" he asked. "From the Cruiser window."

"Tall," she said. "At least nine feet. Possibly nine and a half."

He breathed out through his nose and found the small humor he kept for bad ideas that had to be run anyway.

"Great. I can't wait. Hope you get a clean placement when you take the shot."

"I will do my best," she said, settling behind the scope again.

"Going into the tent," he said over comms.

"Copy," Beretti replied.

He set the chair and lantern inside the tent and sat, a dim shape pretending to read under a low glow.

"On the ledge a woman lay in mud and shadow with glass on the flat. Between them the gully went still, waiting for the first move."

CHAPTER 28

Late heat bled off fast. The light went quick, bright to dim in minutes, and the air slid from warm to cool across her skin. Beretti shifted to take the sting out of her hip and rolled her head until the tightness left her neck. She dropped the night-vision goggles, tuned the focus, and blinked into green. Grain snowed across the lenses, then settled. Her pulse made a soft tick in the rubber eyecups. The tent sat as a soft box below, the lantern set low inside. Small shapes worked their nightly paths along the gully edge, pausing to taste the air and moving on.

"Comms check," Jacobi whispered.

"Clear," she said. "Do not move unless I tell you. I need a clean shot."

"Understood," he said. He lay inside the tent with his phone loose in one hand to sell the scene, sidearm and rifle beside him, ready.

Beretti settled the rifle into her shoulder, bipod firm on rock. She watched the tea-tree line where crawlspace met open dirt. Lantern light breathed through the nylon and sketched the chair and cooler in weak amber.

The gully tightened. Then it broke.

A dark mass burst from the scrub and crossed the clearing low, belly close to dirt, limbs splayed, elbows high, hands striking and driving. Too fast for a clean shot. It slipped behind the tent into the blind pocket where she had no angle.

"Left side. Fast. Behind you," she breathed.

"Copy," he said, voice a hair tighter.

INSIDE THE TENT

The lantern threw a soft square on the fabric. Jacobi stared at the glow and kept still because still read as safe. Somewhere just outside the wall a sound started. A clicking. Not teeth. A dry clatter deep in the throat, quick then slow, like pebbles tapped together in a fist. It moved along the canvas and stopped near his shoulder. The sound raised the hairs on his arms and ignited something primal in him. His body locked down, every nerve leaning forward, braced for a hit he could not see coming.

The charge came low and fast from directly behind the tent. A heavy hit took the rear pole and the whole skin snapped forward. Claws raked the nylon, opening three clean tracks. A second swipe tore a guyline and the canvas sagged. The lantern toppled and went out. Dark punched in.

He rolled for the pistol. A sweep hit the wall and knocked the sidearm from his hand. Fabric pressed to his face. Weight pinned his hips. The breath under the tent stank of rot and old meat.

The rifle was pinned under the collapsed wall, useless. The earbud ripped free in the crush and vanished in the folds. Over his own breath he heard a raspy, rattling breathing close to the fabric, wet at the end. A soft tear of nylon slid inches away, hard to tell left or right. He lifted his forearm and braced. The rake landed across sleeve and skin. Heat flared. He swallowed the sound and held still while thin lines of blood found his wrist. The tent leaned down. A wet nose pressed through the cloth at his cheek and drew a long breath, testing for warmth and life. It traced along his shoulder and neck. Nails scissored again, caught and popped a seam. Cold air poured across his skin.

There was no room to move. No sightline. He pulled his knees under, planted his boots, and kept one thought clear. If it laid flat on him or sat on him it would break every bone in his body.

BACK ON THE LEDGE

Beretti watched the tent buckle and felt the useless urge to fire through cloth. No shot without risking him. Two heartbeats to choose. She chose.

She whistled, loud and shrill.

The mass froze. The head lifted toward the sound, away from the tent line. Clean lane. In the green of the goggles its face was uglier than she had imagined.

She took the first shot on her exhale. The rifle cracked. The round drove through the left eye and out the back of the skull. Before it knew it was dead, she rode the recoil and drove the next into the throat. Cartilage burst, vertebrae snapped, and a dark wash emptied down its chest. The spine was torn. All the strength left it in a single slackening and the body fell backward with its legs still under itself. The tent skin sagged and went still.

"Target down," Beretti said, already moving. "Repeat. Target down."

Safety on. Goggles stayed down. She dropped into the path she had marked with tape and took the slope as fast as the rock allowed. The stink met her halfway, rot and death thick on the air. On the flat she kept the green world steady until her boots hit even ground, then lifted the goggles to clear her depth.

Jacobi had shoved the tent aside and crawled clear, chest working hard where the lantern had died. He checked his arm and hissed through his teeth. Long shallow scratches crossed his forearm and bled in thin streams.

"You good?" she asked, rifle steady, eyes never leaving the shape.

"Yeah," he said, still catching breath. He looked at the blood and shook his head once. "Cosmetic."

"Let me double check."

She circled wide to keep the muzzle on and the wind in her face. Up close the size owned the ground. Shoulders like a rigger's. Back roped with muscle. Hair matted with leaf and clay. Blood ran from the head and neck into the dust. The chest did not move. She reached with gloved fingers to the throat. No pulse. Pupils fixed.

"Dead, twice over," she said.

Her hands started to shake now that it was over. She let them, then set the rifle back on target.

Jacobi pushed to his feet, still panting. He brushed nylon from his shoulders and touched the scratches again, more annoyed than hurt. "It came straight for the blind side," he said, voice rough. "Smart."

"Curious and fast," she said.

"Good thinking with the whistle. Hearing those cracks was a relief."

"You're welcome," she said, patting his shoulder.

Jacobi studied the dead Yowie. "Not far off a Sasquatch, just a bit more Neanderthal through the brow," he said. "Right side of the chest, your hit from last night. See the dried blood matted in the hair. The edges are ragged."

Beretti glanced over at the body then pulled her phone, took wide shots and close details, then dropped a pin on the map and typed a short message to ASIC Ward with the coordinates and a request to send a team to secure the site and take the body. She attached the photos and hit send.

They held where they were, eyes roaming, listening. A hand worked open and closed until the bleed eased. Then the bush exhaled and the night sounds returned.

EPILOGUE

Two days later a maintenance crew unlocked the gate at Bangera Dam to check the spillway. The storm had pushed the level down just enough that air moved through the concrete tunnel under the entry road and brought a heavy, stale smell with it. They called it in.

By the time the sun got above the trees, Haines was on the shoulder with uniforms, SES and forensics working in quiet lines. A pole light slid into the tunnel, the beam washing algae and old flood marks. On a dry shelf above the trickle lay the two young women, pulled clear of the water and covered with brush and grape netting dragged from somewhere else. It looked set, not tossed. They marked the gouges on the concrete lip where something heavy had been hauled across, then brought the girls out with the quiet, methodical care you'd use if their families were watching.

Haines called Jacobi and he answered on the second ring. Beretti stood beside him and listened.

"We found them," Haines said. "Spillway under the road. I've informed the families. I should have been around more while you were here, but you took care of the problem no one else could. Thank you."

"Sorry for the families," Jacobi said. "I'm glad they're found."

"We will carry it from here," Haines said. "You did what you came to do."

Not long after, Beretti's phone lit with a message from Erin: *Thank you. The kids and I slept through the night for the first time in a long time.*

Ellis met them at the bakery that afternoon. She came in on a crutch, brace under her jeans, chin up. A bloke in hi-vis caught the door and eased it wide for her. The woman at the counter had a bag ready before she reached the till.

"How's the leg?" Jacobi asked as she sat.

"Sore," Ellis said, easing into the chair. "Physio reckons a few weeks on the hop, then I should be right." She managed a small smile, let it fade. "That night changed me. I knew the stories, read the files. Seeing it was different. I don't know how you do this."

Beretti took a bite, set the pie down, and wiped her fingers. "You get used to it, surprisingly enough."

Ellis looked between them. "You two make it look simple. It is not. Do you know what made it change how it acted around people? Why it went after homes and then those girls?"

Jacobi shook his head. "Sometimes we never find out the reasoning and why. Pressure builds. Territory shifts. A trigger we never see. We work with what is in front of us."

Ellis nodded, not happy, but accepting the limits.

They ate while the shop filled and emptied. Two tradies argued about football without looking up from their phones. A kid at the counter asked for extra sauce like it was a given. For a few minutes the day felt like any other.

Back at the house they packed. Beretti folded field clothes and slid her notes into a folder. Jacobi rinsed the last mud from his boots and set them by the door. He picked up the Stinger keys from the table and turned them once in his hand.

"Does ASIC Ward know you hired a Stinger?" Beretti asked, one brow up.

Jacobi grinned and turned to her. "No, but I am sure he will."

Their phones buzzed at the same time. Ward.

Change of plans. Currumbin Valley next. South. Dogmen, ongoing problem. I'll send the brief. Take that shiny red Kia you splurged on. Highway Patrol loves those.

Jacobi looked up. "Ah shit. Busted."

Beretti laughed. "Let's grab some coffee, then hit he road," she said, zipping her bag.

He shouldered his pack and pocketed the keys. "One more pie for the drive?"

"Now you are talking."

They hung the keys on the hook, pulled the door shut, and stepped into the warm afternoon. The hills sat blue beyond the roofs. South lay the valley and whatever waited there. The Stinger waited at the curb, engine ticking over.

Beretti slid into the driver's seat. Jacobi buckled in and

said, "Do me a favor: let's not make friends with every speed camera in Queensland."

She smiled, dropped it into drive, and pointed the nose toward the highway.

ABOUT THE AUTHOR

 Luka T. Jacobs, an author from the picturesque Illawarra region south of Sydney, Australia, is passionate about cryptids like Sasquatch and Dogman. She lives there with her partner and their dog, Finnigan.

Luka's love for animals and adventure fuels her storytelling. With a background in Graphic Design and Art, she adds a unique visual flair to her work. An avid traveler and explorer, she draws inspiration from the wild, eager to share her imaginative worlds with readers.

Luka T. Jacobs

Follow on Facebook & join my newsletter for new books, extras, and cryptid goodies.

FB: https://www.facebook.com/lukatjacobs
A: https://amazon.com/author/lukatjacobs
W: http://www.LukaTJacobs.com

Dear Reader,

Thank you for diving into my book amidst a sea of choices,
it truly means the world to me.

If you enjoyed the story, I'd love it if you shared your
experience with others and left a review. As an independent
author, your voice helps bring these tales to life for more
readers, and every recommendation makes a
tremendous impact.

Thank you again for joining me on this journey.
I'm so grateful to have you as a reader!

SNEAK PEAK:
VALLEY OF THE DOGMEN
A NICOLE BERETTI THRILLER

Col Price ran this road most weeks, Casino through the dark folds toward the coast and back again, unload, reload, keep the ledger tidy. Mid-forties, not a big bloke, wiry through the shoulders, and he could put a forty-tonne set exactly where he wanted it. He liked the quiet hours. They let him practise his singing the way he liked it, no audience but the cab and the bitumen. He took karaoke at his local seriously, kept a little list in the glove box, and worked the tricky bits between towns.

The dash clock read 3:42 a.m. A car and truck here and there slid past and was gone. He was just outside Currumbin Valley, near the New South Wales and Queensland border, with the highway mostly to himself. He eased the rig along the two-lane, sat on the limiter, and let the kilometres come. He knew which bends held damp and which fell away on the outside, where fog pooled and where wallabies liked to chance their luck. Just before a blind corner the road washed red. Temporary lights. Rockfall control. He rolled off, took a gear and then another, and brought the truck up square on the line. He could not see the facing green around the bend.

"What's this about," he said to the cab. "No flaggie, no crew. Just a bloody red light in the middle of woop woop."

He thought about running it, pictured the fine and the grief, and let the thought go. "Yeah, right. The missus would kill me."

He always ran with the windows down on this stretch; air off the trees kept his head clear. He cracked his thermos, took a swallow that sat harsh on an empty gut, and set it back in the cradle. The truck made its small, steady noises: fan on low, compressor whisper, the breath of diesel through the firewall.

A clicking started up, light and irregular. He ignored it at first, put it down to motor noise, leaned to the passenger mirror, then the driver, back again, saw only the white posts and the dark seam of trees.

"Hurry up," he told the red. "No one's bloody coming."

He tapped the wheel with two fingers, a little faster

each time.

He rubbed his face, felt the sandpaper of a long week, pressed a knuckle into his eye until the tired shifted. The click came again, closer now. He leaned toward the passenger mirror and tried the little convex spotter. The red threw a hard bubble and stopped. Beyond it, nothing took a shape he could name.

"Come on," he scoffed. "Green. Any day now."

The passenger handle lifted a fraction and dropped, lifted again and held. Not a knock. A try. The door rubber puckered and smoothed. Col's hand shot to the lock and felt it already down. The handle rose a third time and settled. The lock held. One clear thought he did not like crossed his mind: who the hell is out here in the dark.

An arm came through the open passenger window. Long forearm, heavy with dark hair, skin grey where it showed, claws like cracked horn. Hot breath hit his cheek, and with it a stink of wet dog, old urine, and something rotten. It lodged high in his nose and would not shift.

The movement filled the window and he looked.

The face dropped into view. It hunched on the step to fit the frame. Muzzle inches from him. Eyes black and aware.

Lips peeled to show a tearing mouth. Strings of saliva hung and swung with its breath. It stared at him like it was weighing cuts.

Col screamed. No words. He hit the horn with his left hand, jammed the stick with his right, and dumped the clutch. The light might still have been red. He did not care.

He reached behind his seat for the bat he kept there and swung across the cab. Awkward angle, no room. The thing held the step and reached deeper. It caught his forearm as he struck and raked him from wrist to elbow in one hot line while the truck leapt forward. Blood pattered on the mat. He kept the horn talking and drove.

He saw the cut stone wall and fed the truck into it. Mirrors folded. Steel shrieked. The passenger side took the hit and kept taking it. Sparks spat along the door. Dents stamped deep. He bared his teeth and roared over the horn, "Get the fuck off my truck."

A high, sharp cry split the window, pain more than anger, and the arm tore free. The face vanished.

He straightened and kept his eyes on the lane and the mirrors, ignoring the blood running warm down his hand. The door chime pinged where the latch had shifted. Cones flicked under the trailer and popped back up behind. In the mirror a shape kept pace for three long strides on two legs, then peeled into the trees. The stink stayed in his nostrils all the way to the coast.

He did not breathe properly until street lights showed and the ocean smell cut through the cab. At the depot he rolled in crooked and sat with the engine ticking, heart punching. For a moment he tried to convince himself he imagined it. Long night. Bad coffee. Just a wild dog. Maybe it was not what he thought.

Then the pain came on clean.

He climbed down and saw what the stone had done to the truck and what the claws had done to him. The whole left side wore a long scrape and fresh dents, with blood smeared along the panel in a dark handspan where it had ridden the metal. Three deep gouges tracked the passenger door. Two wiry dark hairs stuck in the window seal. Blood dripped from his wrist to his knuckles and made small stars on the concrete.

He leaned against the tyre until the shaking eased. Another truckie came up from a bay, eyes taking in the panel, the blood, the way Col was holding himself.

"You all right, mate?" the bloke asked, closer now. "Are you okay?"

Col did not look up. "I... I don't know," he said.

"*VALLEY OF THE DOGMEN,
A NICOLE BERETTI THRILLER*"
IS COMING NOVEMBER 2025.